The Lost Heir

WITHIN THE CASTLE GATES BOOK THREE

CANDEE FICK

Contents

Dedication

To all those who believe in fairy tales...
But don't feel like royalty.
This castle series is for you.

Become a part of my family of readers and get a FREE novella plus access to exclusive bonus materials. Sign up on my website CandeeFick.com

Prologue

Mid-March 1790, Belgrave Manor

B reaking her fast alone still took getting used to.

However, alone was a relative statement for the liveried footman standing at attention beside the breakfast room's ornate sideboard gave credit to her meticulous hostess, Lady Beaumont.

Mrs. Armstrong swallowed her sip of tea and returned her china cup to the saucer before picking at the usually tempting morsels on her plate. She forced herself to take a bite.

And then another.

She needed her strength for the days ahead.

Oh, if only her Ned were here then she could lean on him in this time of horrific loss.

She blinked away the sudden rush of tears.

How could it be true? Shouldn't her heart have sensed the trouble long before the news finally reached her last eve?

And yet a fortnight had passed since the fire at the coaching inn in Wheatley had left her an orphan, claiming the lives of her parents and siblings. Almost a fortnight since their mass funerals. And over a fortnight since she'd penned the letter to Ned in London announcing her change of plans.

Why hadn't he come or at least sent word? What business was keeping him away?

Pray heaven that his time in town among those of rank had not turned his head or filled him with regret over her simpler upbringing.

The sharp pain squeezing her chest spread to her enlarged midsection and she set down her fork in order to rest her hand atop the increasing evidence of their child.

With weeks to go before her confinement, she'd been the logical—albeit last minute—substitution to serve as companion during her aunt's convalescence after a fall.

But mending a broken bone was simpler than mending a broken heart. And what cruel irony to have escaped mere rumors of a spreading pestilence when the real danger had been an unswept chimney that doomed the inn's inhabitants to a fiery fate.

Leaving her with a widowed aunt and her precious Ned as family.

If only he was near to offer comfort and prayers on her behalf.

She would ask Lady Beaumont to send a messenger to his family's London home posthaste, but such a request must wait until they were settled over their embroidery in the drawing room.

After all, since her injuries, the lady of the house took a breakfast tray in her rooms and only admitted her lady's maid into her inner sanctum.

And today her hostess was equally burdened with her own grief.

"M'lady?"

She glanced up to see the butler near her elbow with a folded newspaper presented on a silver tray.

"Perhaps something to distract you from your woes?"

"Indeed." She swallowed hard and reached for the offering. "I thank you for your kindness."

Living amidst such luxury and exercising the required formalities had been an adjustment, but her mother's sister had married well and after her husband's untimely death, Lady Beaumont was left a proper estate complete with a household of servants and an annual income. And as the lady's niece, the inevitable lessons in proper decorum would serve her well in the future. Ned would surely be pleased at the change.

She unfolded the paper and began to read while sipping on a fresh cup of tea. The first reports were from the House of Lords followed by the House of Commons and by the time she'd finished her tea, she'd turned the page to such items as a salary for the speaker and the consideration of a large bounty for surgeons on slave ships if they provided proof that no more than two slaves in each hundred taken onboard perished.

Her stomach revolted at such a situation and she moved to the next report of mutiny onboard the HMS Bounty. How could God fearing sailors not only defy their authority but set them adrift with meager provisions to fend for themselves against the tides and the natives?

Another harsh cramp beset her and she breathed slowly through the pain that had spread to her lower back.

Already burdened by her grief, the heavy news of the world was too much to bear. Perhaps a lighter distraction?

As the tension eased, her eyes skimmed the page, falling upon the notice of an estate being sold at auction. A reward being offered for the return of a lost greyhound. And an employment posting seeking shoemakers.

Yes. The mundane aspects of life.

She smiled and turned the page yet again, eventually locating the marriage announcements and other items of society gossip.

Her aunt would enjoy dissecting the matrimonial news over their stitching.

Midway down the first column was the news that the banns had been read for the Earl of Wiltshire.

Her eyes widened. A man on his deathbed made for an unusual groom.

A whisper escaped her lips as she read on. A small private ceremony was planned in deference to the recent tragedies in the family. The bride was previously betrothed to the Viscount Lewisham.

She held her breath. The viscount's death in a hunting accident a month ago was the reason Ned had left her side in the first place.

The announcement continued. In addition to grieving the loss of his father and two elder brothers, the Sixth Earl had recently lost his first wife in a fire...

"No!" She pushed back her chair and jumped to her feet. "It cannot be."

The footman rushed to her side. "M'lady?"

A vicious pain sliced across her abdomen and she clutched the edge of the table as a flood of warm liquid washed over her feet.

Tears burned her eyes and she panted for breath. "Dear God. It's too soon for the babe..."

Chapter One

August 1812, Armston in Yorkshire

"Oh, Papa, whatever will I do without you?" Kathleen Harris smoothed a woolen blanket over the severely injured man. He'd been lying abed ever since the trio of men had carried him through the vicarage doors last evening.

Pain-glazed eyes stared out from a too-pale face. "All things work together for good, my child."

"Even getting trampled by a runaway cart?" Her voice trembled.

He had been in the village visiting parishioners when witnesses said he'd pushed a mother and small child out of the way. Saving their lives only to suffer in their place with broken bones and internal injuries.

"Even this." He shifted on the pillows and grimaced. "I fear my time is coming to an end."

"You have survived the night. Who is to say God will not grant you more time?" She blinked away her welling tears.

After his examination, the physician had withheld all hope, then departed. Leaving Kathleen to spend the midnight hours at her father's bedside seeing to his comfort, whispering her love, and listening to his prayers.

"If only I could speak to the earl, then I could be at peace."

"Lord Wiltshire?" If rumor be true, the noble never visited the region, leaving only a skeleton staff to maintain his family's vacant estate on the road to Addingham and a steward to collect the rents.

"Aye. Wiltshire." A flash of a smile hinted at the vitality she knew so well from evenings spent reading in his study while he debated various topics with his latest student. "My patron."

Ah. With the reminder of the semi-annual reports from the vicar to a London address, the deeper implication of her father's impending death settled upon her shoulders. "Because of the living."

The income and the only home she'd ever known would be given to the next man to fill her father's role.

"No. Not the living. Because of you." He grasped her hand atop the blankets and she savored the touch. "I would see you settled. I know you hoped to have the banns read with our young Mr. Cooke in a month's time but..." His expression shifted with a slight frown.

She'd seen the same whenever he weighed his words. In his role as parish vicar, there were many confidences kept and protected. He could not say more.

"I understand."

His lips twisted. "Nothing gets past you, my dear one. I can only say I'd be proud to call him son, but there's...a matter of a rightful inheritance to consider along with a betrothal contract."

As a man granted a living from his benefactor, she'd always known he had no real dowry to give but she was content to be a weaver's wife. And more than content to pledge her life to her handsome friend no matter their income.

"Last week I wrote my old friend to ask his coming that I might seek his advice, but now it seems I may be absent when he arrives."

Was it possible his old friend and the mysterious earl were one in the same? He'd never said as much. And yet, if there was a personal history, he might request a special gift to aid her impending marriage.

Oh, how her curiosity begged for answers to the riddle.

Drops of perspiration dotted on her father's forehead.

Signs of a fever? Her stomach twisted as she reached for a damp cloth and dabbed them away.

With a sudden surge of strength, her father stopped her ministrations and pointed across the bedchamber to a small writing desk. "Kathleen, in my desk. The middle drawer. Two sealed letters for after I'm gone. Letters I'd never dreamed would be needed so soon..."

Gone. A spasm closed her throat at the knowledge that day would come sooner than she'd like.

His eyes widened frantically. "Are they still there?"

If she could ease his mind, he might be able to rest.

Setting aside the cloth, she rose from her chair and crossed the room to the small desk her mother had once used for personal correspondence. It bore little resemblance to the massive furniture in the study downstairs where her adopted father prepared his sermons and tutored bright young men.

She opened the drawer and beside a small stack of fresh paper found two folded and sealed letters. One addressed to the Earl of Wiltshire and the other to her.

The noble and the foundling.

What matter of man wrote to both? Only one who served the Almighty by serving his fellow man, even to his death.

She blinked back the emotion and with letters in hand, returned to her father's side. "They are here."

He relaxed into the pillows as if suddenly weakened. "I sensed an urging these past weeks to put my affairs in order. Now, put the letters in a safer place until I'm gone." He closed his eyes. "I know you are of age and not in need of a legal guardian. However, after he reads my letter, I pray the earl will advise you and see to your wellbeing in my absence."

How could another replace the one whose advice she had always depended upon? And yet, she knew wisdom was needed, especially after a loss.

"I will do as you say." Kathleen reached out to reassure him and felt the alarming heat in his arm. A feverish reaction to his injuries bespoke an infectious element, just as the physician had warned would signal the beginning of the end.

She swallowed her fears. "Rest. I will put these in my room and return to read to you."

"The Psalms, if you please."

"Of course." With a swish of her skirts, she rose and exited the room, crossing the hall to her bedchamber. Two steps past the door, she changed her destination from her desk to the wardrobe and the small wooden chest inside.

He asked for safekeeping and what was more secure than her personal treasure box?

Underneath the intricately carved lid lay a man's mono-grammed handkerchief, a silk shawl, a satin baby gown, and an illegible letter with water stains that had ruined the ink.

She placed the vicar's letters alongside all that remained of her life before being found as an infant on the vicarage doorstep over twenty years before. While Vicar Harris and his beloved wife had not brought her into the world, they had been all the family she needed.

And the kind of family she one day hoped to emulate with her Reuben once they were wed.

Minutes later, she returned to her father's side only to find him mumbling in a feverish state. As she dampened a cloth in the bowl of water, she caught the name Helena.

His wife. The precious woman who had been a mother to Kathleen until her last confinement had sent her to a destination in the graveyard buried with their long desired but regretfully stillborn children.

Kathleen dabbed his brow with the cool cloth while reciting the Psalms from memory for her eyes were too tired and tear-filled to read.

An hour later, when he slipped into an exhausted sleep, she sank onto the chair with an aching back that rivaled the pain of her heart, then bowed her head to offer prayers for a peaceful passing and for her future.

"Miss Harris?"

The sudden voice startled her and she turned to find Mrs. Jennings, their housekeeper, bearing a luncheon tray.

Kathleen's stomach churned. "I'm not—"

The woman bobbed her head as she set the tray aside. "I understand, but perhaps some fresh air would do you good, dear. I'll sit with him for a few minutes if you like." The aged woman and her husband had served the vicarage for longer than Kathleen had been alive.

As much as she wanted to linger by his bedside, a brisk walk would give her energy to face the final hours. "I will not be long."

"Aye, miss." The woman took Kathleen's place beside the sickbed.

Kathleen brushed tears from her cheeks and retreated downstairs to fetch her bonnet and a jacket before venturing out of doors.

Breathing deep of the scent of heather drifting down from the moors, she crossed the lawn toward the hedge gate and soon strolled along the dirt lane that wound alongside the River Wharfe.

As she neared the outskirts of Armston, she paused. It would not do to come upon any of the village housewives while wearing yesterday's wrinkled and stained gown. While some might eye her bedraggled appearance with pity, others would surely judge her for leaving the vicarage at all.

She was well acquainted with their whispers.

However, being perceived as a curious bluestocking who did not adhere to village expectations was nothing compared to the impending loss of her father.

She'd been gone from his side long enough.

She turned on her heel and began the journey back toward the vicarage and the only home she'd ever known. What would become of her as she went from foundling to orphan? Outcast? Alone?

Oh, if only Papa had not acted so heroically then she might be happily planning a wedding instead of dreading a funeral.

Yet if he hadn't, there might have been a different service at the graveyard in a day's time.

At the rattle of wheels and clop of hooves on the rocky road behind her, she stepped closer to the hedge to make room.

"Ho, there."

Her heart skipped at the familiar voice and she turned in time to see Reuben halt the wagon, then jump down from the driver's box. For him to be on this side of the village, he must have been planning to call on her between deliveries.

A few quick steps later, he stood in front of her with work-tousled dark hair above bright green eyes that shone with love...and then compassion. He reached for her hand. "How is he?"

Her tears welled again. "Not long for this world." Her knees shook.

Ignoring propriety, he pulled her into his arms. "My dearest, I will miss him, too." His voice quivered and he took a moment to compose himself. "We may have to wait for the banns to be read, but rest assured that I will do all I can to provide for you for the rest of our lives."

She clung to his strength, nestling against the course fabric of his shirt and sheltered by his broad shoulders as she drew courage from the depth of their love. Her best friend had become so much more over the years of evening tutoring sessions at the vicarage.

"You will always have a home with me and my mother." Reuben's vow brought a wobbly smile to her face.

Despite the speculation spread by the village gossips about the lovely widow, Mrs. Cooke had always treated everyone with equal kindness. And even as she worked long hours spinning and weaving the wool from their sheep to provide for her son until he was of age to take over the income earning, she'd never been one for bitterness.

The Cooke cottage on the other side of the village had been a welcome refuge. If only it could become her home under happier circumstances.

For with or without the vicar's death, she was destined for a simple life. And despite the never-answered questions regarding her true heritage, she would never need to leave the security of Armston.

Never be separated from the man she loved.

She gave Reuben a slight squeeze, then eased back to a proper distance.

A shout came down the lane. "Miss Harris, come quickly." Mr. Jennings ran toward them.

"I'll drive you." Reuben practically tossed her onto the driver's box then jumped up beside her, whipping the horse into motion faster than she could have covered the distance on her own.

The difference a month's time would have made.

Reuben Cooke sat solemnly beside his mother among the other mourners in the church as the visiting curate read the scriptures.

Across the aisle, Kathleen Harris sat apart from the villagers as the departed vicar's sole family with the loyal Jennings relegated to the row behind her as befitting their servants.

With her more-red-than-blonde hair pulled back in a low knot, her black dress made her normally porcelain skin even paler. But despite seeing only her profile, he could still remember the dark circles beneath her green eyes when she'd entered. And the redness from her weeping.

Another month and he'd have had the right to be at her side as her husband with her leaning on his arm. If it wasn't for the strict rules of society, he'd be there now.

Instead, despite his honest conversations with her father about his intentions, the banns had not been read even a single time, and thus he was required to keep his distance. And beyond the inconvenience of waiting for a new clergyman to be assigned to their parish in order to conduct a wedding, he now faced the additional hurdle of a respectable mourning period before taking Kathleen as his wife.

The visiting clergy began the final prayers.

Soon it would be time to carry the casket to the graveyard and lay his mentor to rest.

Reuben swallowed hard and felt the strangling hold of the uncomfortable cravat at his neck. A shirt and trousers sufficed for normal days, but paying his respects to Mr. Harris demanded the courtesy of his Sunday's best on a weekday.

Truth be told, he'd don the constricting clothes daily for the rest of his life if only to regain the presence and guidance of the only father figure he'd ever known.

And yet, he still had a parent to guide him.

Meanwhile, his lovely and beloved Kathleen would soon be homeless as well as fatherless.

He cast a glance her direction at the hunched shoulders that gave away her distress.

Where would she go? And how would she support herself?

If only there were a way to assume the responsibility for her care without causing the town gossips to shame her. Them. But other than a rash trip north to Gretna Green that would cause an even greater scandal, he could merely offer her funds to stay at the rooming house once a new clergyman claimed the vicarage.

But not only would that sully her reputation as if she were a kept woman, it would require more funds than he had readily available, especially as a sheep farmer who supplied wool for several cottagers to spin and weave into cloth.

He might dream of someday leading a weaving enterprise, but only had enough income to support her under his mother's roof, not to provide a separate household.

Surely their neighbors would understand a hasty marriage in light of her sudden loss of father and home. Did practicality surpass propriety?

A slight cough came near his elbow. His mother's gentle reminder to mind his manners and pay attention to the service instead of staring at Kathleen arrived just in time.

Reuben stood and joined the other pall bearers as they transferred the heavy casket outside to the graveyard, then stepped to the side as others lowered it into the ground.

As the mourners gathered around, he found himself close to Kathleen but kept his hands at his sides, ever aware of the eyes of the village gossips at his back dissecting his every reaction.

He could almost sense the butcher's wife cataloging his grief as if to weigh the depth of his feelings for the vicar...and the vicar's pretty daughter.

He would not give them more fuel today. There were already speculations aplenty over the countless evenings he'd spent in the vicar's study supplementing his village education over the years. Evenings that had cemented his bond with the lovely Kathleen.

Those evenings had also escalated the whispers he'd endured his entire life as a fatherless child in a meddling community. Had his widowed mother finally sought a husband in the equally bereaved vicar? Had she used her son to forge a connection far higher than the persistent advances of the boorish blacksmith?

He still recalled the day he'd asked her intentions only to be told that true love only came along once. Due to a distant relative's bequest that paid for their cottage, she had no true need of additional support and so was content to build a life in the quiet Yorkshire countryside and raise her son.

His stomach twisted with the familiar guilt. His mother never spoke of her husband other than in the vaguest of terms and over the years he'd learned to live with the possibility that he was in fact illegitimate even if he publicly stood by the story of her widowhood.

He would not have been the only such child in the village, but as a loving son, he did his best to spare his mother the additional burden.

A year ago, when he'd first declared his feelings for Kathleen, he'd also confided in her his fears about his sullied background lest they become an impediment to a marriage.

In response, his dear friend had chuckled. *I'd be a hypocrite to hold such against you since I know not my own true parentage. We can only be ourselves and live uprightly this day.*

It was the same message the vicar told him many times. To not let the past define him but instead live as one who answered ultimately to the Creator.

Since the source of such advice was now taken too soon, he would need to write such past advice down in a journal so he did not forget the years of imparted wisdom.

He could almost hear the man's voice once again telling him the measure of a true gentleman lay in the heart and not in an entailed estate. If such was the measure, Mr. Harris had been a king among men.

One Reuben resolved to emulate even in the midst of their humble village with a workman's living. All so he could be the man deserving of Kathleen's affections.

He shifted on his feet as the curate uttered the committal, entrusting the vicar to God's care.

"Ashes to ashes, and dust to dust…"

Reuben clung to the promise of the resurrection as the funeral concluded. Handfuls of dirt and a few sprigs of rosemary were dropped onto the casket, and the other parishioners began to scatter.

He stepped to Kathleen's side. "My condolences, Miss Harris."

She nodded, then swayed on her feet.

Reuben quickly offered his arm as support. "May I escort you back to the vicarage?"

"Of course." She placed a trembling hand on his arm, then glanced at his mother with tears glistening in her eyes. "Will you accompany us, Mrs. Cooke?"

His mother nodded and fell in on his other arm as they made their way along the road toward the empty vicarage.

But as they rounded the bend, he spotted a carriage parked outside the gate. Two matched white horses stood in the harnesses and a coat of arms was proudly displayed on the polished wood of the door. A man with a black jacket with shining gold buttons, sparkling white breeches, black hose, and black boots stood awaiting their approach.

Kathleen came to a halt at the sight of the visitor and his mother gasped.

The man advanced with crisp steps. "Miss Harris?"

"I am she." Kathleen's voice wavered and yet she didn't seem as surprised as his mother to see the elegant conveyance.

The man snapped a quick bow. "His Lordship, the Earl of Wiltshire, sends his condolences and this message. He is to arrive at Armstrong Park on the morrow." He pulled a folded parchment from inside his jacket and held it out.

Kathleen continued on toward the messenger to accept the folded missive.

"I will return at noon tomorrow to collect you." With another quick bow, the man turned and retreated to the carriage.

Leaving Reuben with the unsettling realization that more than mere space and grief now separated him from his almost betrothed.

Chapter Two

C ollect her? As if she was a parcel to be commanded at the whims of an absent earl?

Then again, she had been the one to send word of her father's passing along with his sealed letter.

Kathleen eyed the expensive paper in her hand and the ornate seal pressed into the red wax. It was probably an invitation to tea to discuss her living arrangements. She sighed. As if she'd be good company but at least her father had taught her proper manners since she served at his hostess when entertaining guests at the vicarage.

A role she would no longer occupy.

The ever-present grief weighed on her shoulders at the reminder.

Mrs. Cooke prodded her into motion and settled Kathleen upon the settee in the parlor. The next hour passed as she received those who came to pay their respects and partake of a dinner of cold meats and tea served by Mrs. Jennings with the help of Reuben's mother.

At long last, the crowd of villagers thinned.

"Are you not going to read it?" Reuben sat on the straight-back chair to her left and pointed to the missive lying forgotten in her lap.

How could she have forgotten? "Oh, yes." She broke the seal and unfolded the thick paper to reveal a strong handwriting that reminded her of her father's penmanship.

She swallowed the rising emotions and began to read.

Per her father's wishes as evidently outlined in his letter, the earl was declaring himself her temporary guardian and moving her to his estate posthaste. He would send a carriage at noon on the morrow. While she was free to bring any personal and sentimental items she wished, the remainder of the furnishing would remain with the house to serve the arrival of a temporary curate until the living could be bestowed upon...

Dumbfounded, she lowered the letter. "It's not an invitation to dine or take tea. I'm to move."

"What?" Reuben's voice reflected her own astonishment.

She handed him the letter and stared across the room. She'd thought she had time for packing. Time to find a new place to stay.

The mixture of a sob and a laugh burst from her lips. It seemed she had a place to stay after all. At an elegant estate so far from her customary way of life it might as well be a castle.

Reuben groaned. "For how long? And can he demand such a thing? After all, you are of age and don't need a legal guardian."

She sighed. "True, but how am I to refuse? As he lay dying, Father said he wished for the earl to advise me."

"Couldn't he advise from a distance?" Reuben drove his fingers into his dark hair as agony filled his eyes.

The earl had unknowingly ripped them apart and already feeling the separation from those she loved, she reached for his hand. Instead, Reuben moved to sit beside her with an arm around her back and she turned her head to rest on his shoulder as tears ran down her face.

Mrs. Cooke entered carrying a tea tray, then stopped abruptly. "Son. What are you—" She must have caught sight of Kathleen's tears and Reuben's distress. "What is it, my dears?"

Kathleen waved to the letter Reuben had abandoned on his chair.

The woman set aside the tray and picked up the message. She gasped and sank onto the chair as she read. A few moments, she set aside the life-altering words, then rose to pour the tea. "Perhaps it is God's provision for you during this season."

As if this turn of events was a good thing.

"I'm afraid I don't see it as you do." Kathleen accepted the offering of tea with trembling hands and took comfort in the familiar routine and her mother's china.

Would the set be considered a sentimental item? One of many she had less than a day to pack?

Mrs. Cooke motioned her son back to his former chair and took his place at Kathleen's side. "What is it you fear most?"

"That life. I'm used to walking and simpler clothes." She plucked at her black dress. "Did you see that carriage? And the messenger's clothing. Do you suppose he was a relative of the earl to explain such finery?"

"Likely just a footman."

Her eyes widened. "Just a footman. If his servants dress such, I won't know how to act. Not to mention I've never been there. I'll get lost in such a house. And embarrass the earl and my father's memory in one day. What does he expect of me?"

Mrs. Cooke made a soothing noise. "You are truly lovely and from what I've seen of you as his hostess, Mr. Harris prepared you well."

"But not for anything so grand. Maybe I'll be a servant in his house." She nodded. "Yes. I could manage that."

The woman shook her head. "By claiming guardianship, I assume he means more of you than a life of service."

"But mother, how can you be sure?" Reuben set aside his empty cup and leaned his elbows on his knees. "No one around here has seen him in twenty years. Rumor has it he stays in London or at his wife's family estate in Hampshire."

Mrs. Cooke pinched her lips. "You of all people should know better than to put such credence in rumors." She turned to Kathleen. "The bigger question for this day is how can we help you pack?"

Obviously the personal things in her bedchamber would be the first place to start, and yet... Her gaze traveled around the sitting room. A few pictures caught her eye along with a lace doily atop a table. All her mother's belongings that her father had treasured.

Similar reminders were scattered throughout the vicarage.

And then she remembered the loom set up in the spare room where she'd been practicing in anticipation of a life as Reuben's wife.

"I must go through each room, but I fear there will be too much for a single carriage." She set aside her empty tea cup and rose to gather a few items into a small pile.

"My mother and I..." Reuben cleared his throat. "We can store the excess until such time as you are settled and know more."

His mother nodded. "Of course, my dear. We are at your disposal." She waved a hand at her son. "Perhaps you can fetch some paper to make a list?"

Reuben stood as if eager to escape, then strode quickly from the room, likely in the direction of the study.

His destination was a reminder that she wasn't the only one with sentimental feelings about her home and she vowed that Reuben would not leave empty-handed.

The sun had long set before she finally sank onto the mattress in her room. Morning would dawn despite her misgivings.

However, while Mrs. Cooke had made her excuses for the morrow, Reuben had promised to return in the morn to finish crating up her treasures and take a load to his home on the other side of the village.

From a funeral to the impending upheaval, it had been an emotional day.

"Oh, Papa. I miss you so."

Her eyes fell upon the rosewood carved box in the top of her open trunk of clothing and she recalled the letter from her father's desk. By candlelight, she finally broke the seal and with tears streaming down her cheeks, heard her father's voice in the written words.

My dear Kathleen,

I cannot explain the urgency that my time with you is short and therefore I set ink to paper in a feeble attempt to record the depth of my emotion. Never forget that you are loved.

Aside from the love of my darling Helena, your unexpected arrival on our doorstep has become my greatest blessing. I'm honest enough to admit I had questioned the Almighty about why my beloved and I were not able to have children. But in his goodness, God had already provided us a daughter. In the caring of you, we found peace and a target for our affection. When my Helena was taken too soon, you were there to offer comfort and companionship.

As you know, in the absence of her rigid adherence to social norms, I was given leeway to entertain my whims and allow you to linger in the study while I tutored the village boys including young Mr. Cooke. I pray that your appetite for knowledge, keen insight, and wealth of compassion serve you well no matter where life plants you.

I could not have asked for a more accomplished daughter.

With this unexplained unction to record my thoughts, I have had a corresponding vision of you in elegant finery the such as I would never be able to provide. Perhaps it is a symbol of the life you were always destined for and a sign our time together is drawing to a close.

I'll admit I did not wish to too-closely investigate your origins for fear of losing you from our lives. Forgive me my past selfishness.

Always know that I have always wanted the best life has to offer on your behalf.

If you wish to pursue answers at this juncture, I now wish you well. However, as your father and your vicar, I must also caution that you do not let any pursuit of your heritage negate the reality that you are already a beloved child of the King of Kings. No other title matters as much as that.

You are my precious gift.

With all my love,

Peter Harris

She sighed, then clutched the letter to her chest. Dear Papa had been the one to give her the gift of a home, a family, knowledge, and now his permission to seek her roots.

Perhaps his letter to the earl was his way of providing her the necessary connections to begin her search. Perhaps some good would come from his passing, even if it would never erase her memories of a happy childhood.

She replaced the letter in the box, blew out the candle, and settled beneath her blankets.

Her father and his friend the earl were set on removing her from the village life and placing her on the fringes of society. A place where it was assumed her real mother had at least circulated based on the quality of the fabrics and the intricate stitching on the items found with her.

Were there answers to be found in the wider world of Yorkshire?

As much as it grieved her to leave Armston—and Reuben—behind for at least a season, she could not deny the desire to see more of England and find where she truly belonged.

Reuben braced himself for the most difficult day of his two and twenty years. How did one say goodbye to their heart?

He took a deep breath, then tapped on the door to the vicarage.

A minute later, Mrs. Jennings ushered him inside and gave a small curtsy. "Miss Harris is in the vicar's study."

"Thank you." He nodded his head, then bypassed the stack of trunks set against the wall including one he'd carried down from her bedchamber last eve.

With his mother's help, Kathleen had cleared most of her personal belongings from the other rooms, leaving her father's study for last. It was the room most filled with reminders of her recent loss.

He paused in the doorway to see her perusing the shelves, trailing a slender finger along the spines of the books. As if saying farewell to dear friends.

He cleared the emotion from his throat. "Kathleen."

She turned and a smile blossomed, then wavered. "This room..."

"I understand. How can I help?"

She inhaled, then crossed to stand in front of him. "I decided that you should have his desk."

He glanced to the side and the massive surface covered with two stacks of books.

"Not that one. The earl would likely consider that part of the essential furnishings of the house."

He nodded while pushing aside a twinge of some unnamed emotion. Likely regret, and yet what need had he for such furnishings?

She lowered her voice. "My father had a smaller piece in his bedchamber for personal correspondence and while I do not have need of it, I am sure he would have wished you to have something as a symbol of your lessons. I took the liberty of stocking the drawers with fresh paper and a full ink pot."

Gratitude warmed his heart. "It is much appreciated and I will honor his memory when I sit to write there."

"You were his favorite student." Her lips curled into a teasing smile as she glanced at the cluster of chairs positioned around the fireplace.

"Perhaps because I spent so much time here." Unlike other boys his age and of their humble station, his mother had insisted on expanding his education to rival that of the noble sons who traveled to Eton and Oxford. Something they could not afford but Mr. Harris had been willing to attempt in exchange for a supply of woolen cloth for his clothing and thread for his carpets.

It was a small price to pay for the treasure of knowledge and the vicar's wisdom.

Kathleen rested a hand on one stack of books. "I do not see the new occupant finding much use for Robinson Crusoe or Captain Cook's adventures. Or even the History of the Americas."

He stepped closer. "I still remember when you spoke from across the room to voice your opinion. Put me in my place and challenged me to prove you wrong."

She chuckled. "I *was* correct."

"That time." Eventually Mr. Harris had invited his daughter to join their lessons and the resulting friendship gave rise to feelings of a deeper nature. "I will never forget those evenings together. Nor what we might have had. I wish—"

She pressed a finger against his lips. "Nay. Don't say it. Nothing will change my feelings and I can't bear to lose you too. Besides, Armstrong Park is just down the road and can be seen from your land. We will not be that far apart."

"For now." Unless the earl decided to take her to one of his other estates. But the implied social distance between the Tudor style manor on the hill and the simple village was a chasm he could not fathom how to cross.

"His Lordship likely fancies the change in lodgings a simple act of charity to honor my father. But in time, I hope to change his mind and therefore this imminent separation will not be forever."

Hope swelled in his chest and he nodded. "Then I will consider your crates and the loom being stored at our cottage as assurance of your return for them." *And for me.*

"If I may be so bold, if I am unable to visit in person for some time, would you accept my letters? The delivery of messages from Armstrong Park should not cost more than a pittance."

He grasped her hands and held them over his heart. "Eagerly. And often. You must tell me everything." He smiled to lighten the mood. "Teach me about the world beyond our borders and you will find me a willing student."

"Will you write in return?" She caught her bottom lip between her teeth.

He closed the distance to brush a light kiss across her mouth. "You are my heart and I will never forget you."

A rattle in the hallway outside the open door brought him to his senses and he released his hold on Kathleen. "Rest assured, my dear Miss Harris, that I will put your gift of paper and ink to use regularly."

"I will hold you to your word." Kathleen pressed her fingers to her lips, then to her heart before placing her hand on his chest.

An unspoken vow. Like that of his kiss.

One that would have to suffice until the banns could be read.

A clomping of boots echoed outside the door and after a quick nod to acknowledge her words, he stepped back to insert a proper distance between them. "Now, as time hastens, what is left to be crated?"

Kathleen lifted her chin and turned to the books. "I have already added a few volumes to my last trunk, but would like to store the rest of these at your cottage. Either inside a crate or on a shelf will be left to your discretion."

He fought to contain his smile as he looked forward to revisiting the pages in the evenings to come. "As you wish."

The next hours were spent moving a small stack of baggage to the yard to await the carriage while loading the promised desk and several crates into his wagon. As he and Mr. Jennings wrestled Kathleen's spinning wheel and loom into place, he marveled that Kathleen had been so willing to learn and prepare for a future as a weaver's wife.

Except there would be no use for such tasks at her new home.

Would she outgrow him in the months to come?

Nay. He would work even harder to expand his business. And spend his evenings learning. All so that when her period of mourning was over, he could approach the earl for her hand and bring her back to Armston as his wife.

As promised, the earl's carriage arrived promptly at noon. Followed shortly by a crowd of curious villagers come to gawk at the finery as he and Mr. Jennings helped secure Kathleen's belongings at the rear of the carriage.

In less time than he'd anticipated, she was saying her tearful goodbyes to the Jennings. After a slight wave and curtsy to the villagers, she stopped beside the carriage steps and held out a hand for his assistance.

Because of their audience, he settled for lifting her hand to his lips in a proper but courtly farewell, praying his eyes conveyed his promises. Her eyes shown with equal longing and grief before she entered the carriage and took a seat.

"Godspeed in your journey, Miss Harris."

"And to you, Mr. Cooke."

The footman secured the door, then bounded into place on the driver's box and took up the reins. With a crisp snap, the matched whites sprang into motion and made their way back toward Armston and the manor beyond.

With a burdened heart, Reuben nodded his farewell to the Jennings and soon traced a similar path down the dusty road toward his cottage. Once the wagon bed was unloaded, he'd be about his never-ending tasks delivering wool and receiving thread and cloth from his small network of cottagers.

All the while praying that her time spent in high society would not change his precious Kathleen.

Chapter Three

K athleen pressed a hand atop her stomach as the carriage hit a jarring bump in the road and then settled back into a rhythm. With every turn of the wheels, the horses drew her further from the security of everything she'd once called home.

They'd already passed the Cooke cottage on the outskirts of the village and the rustic countryside spread wide on either side of the road leading to Addingham. Too soon, the carriage slowed enough to turn onto a smoother gravel drive and began to climb the gentle hillside overlooking the River Wharfe.

She held her breath as they cleared a cluster of trees and the relative wilderness of pastures transformed into a lush, well-manicured lawn. Sculptured bushes lined the circular drive leading to the center of Armstrong Park's impressive facade. Two stories of gray stone rose before her with rows of tall windows on either side of the massive front door.

Before she was ready, the carriage came to a stop and the footman was there in an instant to lower the steps and help her down.

"Miss." He nodded his head in deference, then gestured toward the intimidating entrance. "Go on now. The staff will see to your belongings."

If the footman's attire was any indication, the staff were more elegantly dressed than she'd ever been even before donning her black mourning dress.

She forced her feet to move up the wide stone stairs toward her temporary home.

By the time she'd reached the door, the carriage had disappeared around the corner of the manor home, presumably to the servants' entrance.

With no one around, was she just to open the door? Or knock? She scrambled through her memory for proper protocol when at the home of a noble. Except her father's lessons had centered more on geography, history, and philosophy.

Before her panic took full root, the door swung open on silent hinges. Another footman stood to the side and motioned her forward to where another man in formal dress stood at attention in the middle of a grand entryway large enough to house the main floor of the vicarage. A sparkling chandelier cast light over the massive curving double staircase and the polished woodwork.

"Miss Harris." The man offered a polite nod in her direction but his keen eyes swept from her mother's old bonnet on her head down to the tips of her dusty boots.

She dipped into a curtsy, somehow feeling like it was required in the presence of such grandeur and lowered her eyes to the tiled floor.

He coughed. "No need for that. I'm the butler. His Lordship arrived a half hour past and requests your presence in the library at once. If you will follow me."

Heat flooded her face and tears pricked her eyes. If this was the butler, however was she to interact with the earl?

Kathleen folded her hands at her waist and attempted not to gawk at the gilt-framed art and colorful vases of flowers atop antique tables as she trailed behind the butler.

A brisk knock on the wood gave warning and then the butler opened the door. "Miss Harris has arrived, m'lord."

"Show her in." The answering deep voice sounded more weary than irritated so perhaps she wasn't a burden after all.

She moved through the doorway, quickly taking in the floor to ceiling shelves on all sides except for the wall of windows facing the back of the house and offering glimpses of a manicured garden. On the near side of the glass, a cluster of chairs invited her to pass the time with a book. Later. Assuming her self-appointed guardian allowed her access.

At the center of the room, an older gentleman with red hair stood behind a massive desk. With the elaborate folds of lace at his neck in addition to an embroidered green waistcoat set off by a black jacket and breeches, he was obviously the earl.

She dropped into a deep curtsy as was proper. "My lord."

He nodded to acknowledge her even as she felt his gaze sweep over her attire followed by a slight frown. "Miss Harris."

He pointed her to a chair and only then did she notice the ruddy-faced portly man already seated near the desk with a ledger open on his lap.

The earl returned to his seat. "Mr. Finch, my steward, was giving me his account of my Yorkshire holdings." A slight motion of the earl's hand both introduced and dismissed the man.

Mr. Finch's lips tightened in response as if offended.

A heavy silence filled the room, then Lord Wiltshire cleared his throat. "I was surprised to receive your father's letter a week ago requesting my presence in the region and then shocked to learn of his accident as well as his passing before I could arrive. May I offer my sympathy in your time of grief."

"Thank you, m'lord." Her voice cracked.

"I admit to a curiosity and would like to discuss the contents of your father's letters." He gestured to a few open papers on the desktop. "However, since I have much to do before I must return to London tomorrow, it will have to wait until such time as I can return."

He was already leaving? What was to come of her in the meantime?

"You, of course, will stay here." He turned to the steward. "Fetch Mrs. Pembroke if you please."

The man heaved himself out of his chair, deposited his ledger on the desktop, then lumbered toward the door.

"Your father asked for my advice concerning your future, but I can already see that I was correct in my assumptions. I have secured the services of a companion to see to your wardrobe and your lessons."

"Lessons, m'lord? My father assured I was quite knowledge-able in—"

He raised an eyebrow that matched the red tones of his thin-ning hair and she looked down in shame for questioning her superior. "I cannot believe that Mr. Harris taught you proper deportment and the required social graces to make a suitable match."

"A match? But I—"

"You will remain here under her tutelage until you are ready to be presented."

Presented? Where? To whom?

The cascade of change and resulting profusion of questions left her light-headed and glad to be seated.

The library door opened and the steward returned, followed by an elegantly dressed woman with slightly graying hair pulled up into an elaborate bun beneath her lace cap.

The woman sank into a graceful curtsy, then settled herself on the edge of an unoccupied chair, keeping her spine stiff.

Kathleen subtly tried to mimic her posture and immediately felt the strain in her unused muscles.

After conducting the proper introductions, the earl leapt into the matter at hand. "I will expect weekly progress reports to be included with those of my steward. Your aim is for her to be ready to meet the countess, my sons, and the ton after the new year."

Mrs. Pembroke turned her direction as if measuring the extent of work to be done.

The earl grunted and continued. "Finch, you will of course allocate the funds including pin money for both women's incidental needs, but Mrs. Pembroke, spare no necessary expense as you prepare Miss Harris for the Season."

Kathleen squeezed her hands together in her lap. "M'lord? It's too much. Too extravagant."

Lord Wiltshire waved away her interruption. "Nonsense. He may not have said as much in his letter, but I'm sure your father wanted you to see London and the country for yourself before settling down."

His dying words had not given her that impression, but she could easily admit her curiosity to see and experience the greater world.

A minute later, the women were dismissed and the earl resumed his talk with the steward.

In the hall outside the library, Mrs. Pembroke circled her slowly, examining her figure and even lifting Kathleen's chin to peruse her eyes and face. "Passable. We'll have the dressmaker in by Friday to take your measurements."

"Friday? But—" Kathleen's protests were cut off by a stern frown.

"I'll grant you the remainder of the day to get settled in your rooms, but I'll expect you in the drawing room at nine o'clock sharp tomorrow morning to test your knowledge so I know where to begin your lessons."

"I already know—"

"I will not shirk my duties. You will need to prove to me that you know proper etiquette, have memorized the peerage, and have at least some skill with embroidery, music, or painting in addition to household management, hostessing, and of course dancing." The woman raised an eyebrow as if she were knowledgeable of all Kathleen's deficits.

In an instant, Kathleen realized that between her natural curiosity and a mother's absence, she had learned the wrong sorts of things in her father's study. And even though she'd tried to hide her intellect from the village gossips, it seemed they agreed with Mrs. Pembroke.

She would never get a husband with her nose in a book.

"At least the Countess Wiltshire is still at Rotherfield Park in Hampshire." The woman's lips pinched. "However, we certainly have a lot to accomplish in such a short amount of time." She turned and summoned a footman. "Fetch someone to show her to her rooms and order a dinner tray. She will dine alone above stairs until we can fit her with a proper wardrobe."

With a swirl of skirts, Mrs. Pembroke departed, leaving Kathleen standing alone and speechless from the harsh judgment.

Had the woman no compassion?

And yet, Kathleen embraced the challenge.

Surely she could learn the necessary social skills with the same diligence she'd applied to her mathematic exercises.

The footman returned with a woman Kathleen recognized from the back of the church on many a Sunday over the years.

Mrs. Seymour introduced herself as the housekeeper, then after offering her condolences, proceeded to give Kathleen a speedy tour of the ground floor of the house.

In short order, she had become acquainted with the earl's library, the private salon for the lady of the house, the drawing room, the dining room, the breakfast room, and the kitchens. She even caught a glimpse of the dusty ballroom before the housekeeper led her up the stairs chattering away about meal times and a lady's maid.

By the time they reached her guest room in the east wing, Kathleen was completely overwhelmed with information and happy to release Mrs. Seymour back to her duties.

Kathleen shut the heavily carved door and turned to face her new refuge in the months to come. A large canopied bed with rose-colored hangings took up the right side of the room with a fireplace and wingback chair to her left and a wardrobe and dressing screen in the corner. A writing desk stood near the window and two of her trunks were pushed against the gold-papered wall.

Despite simpler furnishings than those she'd seen elsewhere in the house, the luxury of the bedroom made her acutely aware of the dust accumulated during her morning activities and short drive.

As she crossed the thick carpets toward the screen, she removed her shabby bonnet, then rounded the corner to find a washstand with fresh water. After removing the dust from her hands and face, she wandered to the window that overlooked the gardens.

She would have to explore their reaches. Later. Once she'd adjusted to the changes and settled in.

With echoes of Mrs. Pembroke's instructions ringing in her ears, Kathleen opened her trunks to discover that her clothing had already been removed to the wardrobe, leaving only a few personal knickknacks to arrange to her liking and a stack of books.

She took a few minutes to set a doily, framed picture, Papa's paperweight, and her rosewood box on the mantel. A pang of longing pressed upon her heart and she lifted the lid to remove her father's last letter.

I have always wanted the best life has to offer on your behalf.

For now, it seemed the extravagant Armstrong Park, a visit from the dressmaker, and a trip to London were part of that best life.

She returned the letter to its place and lowered her head.

"Papa, I won't forget you even in the midst of this luxury. And I will do my best to learn all I can so that I do not disappoint the earl."

But London?

She'd only read about the capital in the newspapers, especially the ongoing debates about the Napoleonic Wars.

To think that she would see it with her own eyes before long.

What would Reuben think? She would have to immerse herself in the new experiences and share it with him through her letters.

She moved to the desk and pulled out a sheet of paper to begin her first letter.

On the corner of the desk was a copy of a book she'd brought with her thinking it might be useful. The new copy had obviously been placed there by Mrs. Pembroke before Kathleen's arrival.

Hadn't the woman mentioned something about memorizing the peerage?

An idea bloomed, and with a smile, Kathleen reached for the quill.

Reuben adjusted the parcel under his arm, knocked the clods of dirt from his boots, and entered the small cottage he shared with his mother.

At once he was surrounded by the familiar rhythm of the clacking pedals as the shuttle flew through the warp of a loom on his left. They'd turned the larger front room into a workspace and entertained their rare callers in a corner of the kitchen instead.

Practicality over propriety as his mother often said.

He stopped in the doorway to see her at work at Kathleen's newer loom. In his dreams, he'd imagined the two women he loved working together and filling the space with their chatter. But now it felt lonely.

He sighed.

"I miss her too." His mother nodded his direction. "What's that you have?"

He grinned and strode into the room, taking a seat on the stool beside the spinning wheel. "Mr. Harding stopped me during my morning deliveries with a letter and a package from Kathleen."

"Gone but two days and already sending news?" The loom paused. "Well, out with it. What does she have to say about the house on the hill and its master?" A hint of something in her tone that reminded him of his own fear-filled curiosity.

He opened the folded parchment and skimmed past the opening endearments he would revisit later in the privacy of his bedchamber. "She describes a lavish home and claims she is likely to get lost. As for the earl, it seems he stayed only long enough to commend her into the care of a Mrs. Pembroke before departing for London again."

"Indeed." A flash of disappointment washed across her face. "If she needed looking after, I would think Mrs. Jennings could have sufficed with no need to uproot the girl."

"Ah, but apparently she's to be fitted with a new wardrobe and prepared for a debut plus a Season."

His mother gasped. "A Season? Does he mean to marry her off?"

Reuben's stomach churned at the voicing of his ultimate fear, then lifted the letter. "She hasn't said as much but instead focused on the overwhelming list of things she is now required to learn before she can be presented to the countess for approval."

His mother sniffed. "That lovely girl already has all the approval she needs."

"I agree." He swallowed hard, then unwrapped the book she had sent along with her letter. "However, since the stern Mrs. Pembroke provided her with a new copy, Kathleen sent this copy of DeBrett's Peerage for me lest I become remiss in my studies. She found it among the vicar's most recent acquisitions."

His mother eyed the volume as if intimidated by the names it contained.

He sighed. "While she tried to cast things in a positive light, I can sense how unsettled she is about the litany of changes. Meanwhile I can do nothing to help her adjust except pray for her wellbeing and correspond with reminders of home. And now perhaps study these pages."

His mother frowned and a flash of pain crossed her eyes. "What benefit do you see in learning of the noble families when you have no present opportunity to meet any of them? It is Kathleen who will soon be introduced to earls and countesses with the sponsorship of one of their kind."

Would her coming adventure in London put her out of reach and leave him with a broken heart?

He shook off the possibility. "Kathleen won't change." In either her character or the object of her affection. Or at least he hoped. "However, I'm competitive enough to want to memorize the book before she can."

His mother waved a hand at the worktable. "In that case, leave the volume there. I'm curious to see the listings myself and will do my part by quizzing you in the evenings."

"Agreed." He stood, deposited the book, and pocketed the letter. "In the meantime, I've time for a quick luncheon then need to check the flock. Those new sheep I bought this spring may be ready to shear again soon."

He'd read about a breed whose wool could be shorn twice a year and that meant more thread to be woven into carpets instead of cloth.

If the experiment proved worthwhile, he would have another avenue to expand his income but might need to find another weaver.

No doubt about it. If he wished to provide for Kathleen in the style she would soon be accustomed to, he needed more hours in the day, a central location, or a market for his cloth closer to home than Addingham or Leeds.

But as the clatter of the loom resumed and he detoured to the kitchen for a slice of bread and cheese, he could hardly wait until evening when he was free to study Kathleen's book and compose a response.

On paper she'd given him while seated at the desk that was also a gift.

His stomach soured. Receiving charity was difficult to swallow as a man.

Chapter Four

Letter from Kathleen to Lord Wiltshire:

I took the liberty of enclosing this letter with the steward's weekly packet and hope I did not overstep.

When you assigned Mrs. Pembroke the task of my wardrobe, I could never have imagined such a number or variety of fabrics, colors, and styles. I fear my knowledge of fashion was severely deficient. I am overwhelmed at your generosity and humbled to be a part of your extended household for the time being.

Mrs. Pembroke conveyed your wishes about putting aside my mourning clothes once the London Season begins and I'm thankful for the concession of a few simple black gowns until that occasion arises.

While my mornings are spent sequestered in the drawing room, many an afternoon I have enjoyed exploring the gardens and paths before taking tea. From the top of the hill, the vista is especially breathtaking with the white dots of sheep contrasting with the green of the fields and the shimmering thread of the River Wharfe winding through it all connecting one village to the next town and beyond...

Letter from Kathleen to Reuben:

Only to you would I confess the trepidation that ensued upon the delivery of my new wardrobe. I had resisted the assignment of a lady's maid to my care but will soon depend on her expertise to remember the ins and outs of which fabrics and styles are suitable for mornings, calling, riding, dinners, and eventually balls. The variety of colors puts me in mind of a rainbow above a garden of wildflowers.

Although, my favorite so far is a simple white gown that can be altered in appearance with a different colored sash or shawl. It reminds me of my mother's simple style while the intricate pattern of stitching adds a touch of elegance.

While I am indebted to the earl for his generosity on my behalf including an allowance beyond my means to spend, I fear what the villagers and society at large will say about cutting my mourning period short. However, Mrs. Pembroke determined that filling my days with endless lessons and confining my excursions to the immediate grounds were adequate concessions for a daughter in mourning...

Letter from Reuben to Kathleen:

Do not fear what others may say for I am convinced your father would understand your current circumstances. And do not forget the words of Saint Paul concerning those who are asleep, that we sorrow not, even as others who have no hope...

Letter from Kathleen to Reuben:

I am ever grateful for your reminder of the truth of Scripture and rest in the consolation that I will see my father again. As we too will eventually be reunited.

Mrs. Pembroke has lately occupied my days with a full inspection and inventory of the rooms as part of my education in overseeing the proper care of a house. The occupation is not so very much altered from my duties at the vicarage other than the vast number of carpets and drapes to be cleaned and examined for repairs...

Letter from Reuben to Kathleen:

When you wrote of a quantity of carpets, I never imagined you would refer the housekeeper to my address to acquire the necessary thread to perform such repairs. I was equally astonished to be the recipient of a standing order for new carpets.

The acquisition of such a consistent income has allowed me to sign a lease agreement for that abandoned mill building near the river. I now have the means to consolidate a collection of spinners, weavers, and finishers under a single roof.

The location pales in comparison to the worsted mills I observed in Addingham during my last market trip, but the new arrangement will restore hours to my day for instead of traversing the winding roads between cottages, I will only have a short walk from one station to the next.

With my devoted attention to the business, I hope for great things. I have such plans for the future. Our future...

Letter from Kathleen to Reuben:

I am delighted to hear of your new building and when I look down upon the village during my afternoon walks, I can now imagine you and your dear mother within those walls.

I regret not being allowed to attend services at the church each week but admit that seeing another standing in my father's place would bring about fresh grief. I found a book by William Wilberforce in the library for spiritual nourishment. I am challenged by his declaration that a true Christian is one discharging a debt of gratitude to God for the grace he has received. I also gather weekly with the servants for a time of prayer and must consider that enough for the time being.

On a lighter note, I am pleased to report that I successfully applied my recent knowledge of the peerage to Mrs. Pembroke's challenge to arrange the seating of a dinner party in such a manner as not to offend anyone...

Letter from Reuben to Kathleen:

Your mention of dinner parties brought to memory the assembly at the harvest and Mrs. Elkin's claiming of a seat at the vicar's table solely because her husband had contributed to the pew box restoration fund.

Did not our Savior teach us to take the lower seat at a banquet? It is far better to be elevated in position than lowered.

However, where do you suppose stewards fit into such gatherings? While I hesitate to share my frustration in light of your connection to Lord Wiltshire, I had an unfortunate incident with his steward the other day...

Letter from Kathleen to Reuben:

Sharing your frustrations with me is by no means disloyal to the earl. We've known each other for years and I had hoped we were past such restraints. Do not fear speaking the truth.

May I offer my apologies on behalf of the earl for the poor treatment by his steward? I cannot fathom his sneering at one in the position to deliver higher rent payments while in the position of bettering the livelihoods of others.

I am certain you labor far more diligently than he every day. From what I have observed, he freely indulges in the earl's brandy and spends more time at a pub in Addingham than hunched over the ledgers here at Armstrong Park. It is no wonder that tenants usually come to the head gardener for advice and only contact the steward to deliver their rents...

Letter from Kathleen to Lord Wiltshire:

I hesitate to bring the following to your attention, however because of your lavish generosity toward me, I cannot bear to see your good name being maligned by association or your fortune misused.

Last week while I was in the library to retrieve a book for Mrs. Pembroke, I happened upon the unattended estate ledgers lying open upon the desk. Drawing upon my lessons in household management, my curiosity was piqued to see the recorded expenses. To my shock and dismay, I observed a frequent expenditure at the Red Lion Tavern in Addingham. In addition, Mrs. Seymour had revealed to me her secrets for stretching her weekly allotment for foodstuffs and yet the recorded amount in the ledger was twice her stated amount.

Due to the nature of my errand and the sudden return of the steward to the room, I was unable to ascertain the duration of such incongruities.

Forgive my intrusion into matters that do not directly concern me when it comes to the household accounts. However, as a longtime resident of the parish, there is also a general opinion of your representative that equally discredits your reputation as an honorable landowner.

West Yorkshire is known for weaving, especially woolens. However, I know from a reliable source that your steward has stifled all attempts to bring similar prosperity to your tenants. Although one ambitious weaver has contrived a means to circumvent those machinations...

Letter from Mrs. Pembroke to Lord Wiltshire:

As previously reported, Miss Harris continues to be a quick learner and prudent as well. This week alone, she encouraged the housekeeper to seek out a villager to provide the woolen cloth for the servants' livery rather than venture to Addingham or even Leeds to purchase it there. Do not fear. The cloth is of a supreme quality and with the local purchase, the transaction saved the merchant's commission which did much to increase the estate coffers.

After the surprising dismissal and replacement of the former steward, I am pleased to report that such interactions as the one recommended by Miss Harris have also done much to restore and advance relationships with your tenants...

Letter from Reuben to Kathleen:

It seems we have finally been assigned a curate to fill the pulpit regularly although rumor has it the assignment is temporary in nature as the earl has reserved the living for his youngest son once he takes orders. Nevertheless, I wish you were free to attend our humble services again so that I could see you in more than my dreams.

I also wish I could express my gratitude in person for the significant order of cloth for the manor's livery. Mrs. Seymour more than hinted that the purchase came at your suggestion but I am assured she left well pleased and will return in the future.

The profit from the transaction allowed the purchase of additional wool from several of our neighbors and gives me hope that I might be able to explore the installation of a water-powered loom in the new year. I cannot afford such a contraption at present and certainly am not in a position to invest in a steam powered configuration as some in Addingham are attempting. However, the future of weaving is changing and we must improve if we are to compete.

I am enclosing an article on the subject for you to read. I am confident you will share your opinion...

Letter from Kathleen to Reuben:

At long last, a subject that matters. Thank you for providing something of interest to read. The idea is fascinating and I can see how it would benefit the village at large to have the ability to produce more cloth so quickly. Would you purchase raw wool or the finished thread from our neighbors to supplement your enterprise?...

Letter from Kathleen to Lord Wiltshire:

With Christmastide approaching, I desire to make arrangements for the staff to celebrate together, but did not know your intentions. Will I see you before the new year?...

Note from Lord Wiltshire to Kathleen:

Advise the steward and obtain a ten pound allotment to do with as you wish. I will celebrate the twelve days of Christmas with my family. Expect my arrival on the seventh of January. If your progress is indeed as Mrs. Pembroke has reported, be prepared to leave for London shortly thereafter.

Letter from Kathleen to Reuben:

I could not fathom how I would survive this time of year without my father and was so looking forward to your invitation to spend Christmas Day at your home. I pray your dear mother a speedy recovery from her ailment and agree that adding stoves to your new workshop would improve the conditions for all.

I cling to the promise that all things work together for good although I still cannot see the Almighty's purpose in being alone in my celebrations. Perhaps I am meant to bring a bit of cheer to those who serve the earl so faithfully in his absence.

With the dreary weather keeping me indoors, I have dedicated my free hours to wandering the gallery for exercise and finishing my preparations of small gifts for the staff.

Do extend my gratitude to your mother for her aid in securing the fine woolen stockings for the earl. Her craftsmanship is exquisite and I pray he will receive my humble attempt at repaying his kindness in the spirit it is intended.

I admit my trepidation at seeing him again and pray—I seem to be doing that frequently these lonely days—he deems my efforts suitable enough. Whatever shall I speak of during our time together? I know all too well that I have little in common with a man of his rank.

Please accept these gifts with all my heart. I pray you remain in health and that the new year sees us reunited at last...

Letter from Reuben to Kathleen:

My dear Kathleen,

I hesitate to ask where you found such a volume but freely express my appreciation at the information it contains about mechanizing cotton mill operations. I daresay that the applications for wool are clearly on the horizon of innovation and God willing, may eventually traverse the distance from Addingham's enterprise to our humble hamlet.

The only lack in such a generous gift of knowledge was your absence at our table and not simply for the opportunity to debate the merits and faults of such endeavors. My eyes drifted too often to the chair that should have been yours were it not for a drafty warehouse and a week of rain.

As a gift to those in my employ, I have hired young Stephan to fill the cracks and ordered a heating stove to be delivered within the fortnight.

Mother is slowly recovering her strength and just this morning I found her resting before the fire with your gift of a silk shawl gathered about her shoulders.

I regret withdrawing our invitation but could not risk your taking ill and missing your adventure in London. For your own sake and mine. While I would never wish you harm, I selfishly admit a desire for continued correspondence and regular descriptions of the sights and sounds of the city as seen through your lovely eyes.

I understand your fears when you are at last reunited with your guardian-of-sorts. However, did you not tell me he was a childhood friend of your father's? Perhaps you might open a conversation by asking for a story to remember your father by. I pray God guides your words...

Chapter Five

January, 1813, Armstrong Park

K athleen clasped her hands at her waist as she strolled the gallery hall.

Lord Wiltshire's arrival was imminent and she was beset with nerves. And not just about seeing the earl again but about gaining his approval. About traveling with him to London. About meeting the rest of his family.

About not causing him any embarrassment while there.

She perused the formal paintings of the numerous generations who had called this place home.

After five months living under the same roof, she still felt like an outsider.

Perhaps it was merely because her companion was paid to train her and all interactions were therefore properly formal. Or the reminder that while the servants had warmed to her presence during their Christmas celebrations, they knew their place and had retreated full force with the earl's temporary return.

She wasn't a servant or paid employee, but she wasn't family either.

Just a charity case without home or fortune.

Near the end of the hall with the more recent family portraits, she focused on one mother's gold gown. The color complemented the woman's red hair while the yards of detailed brocade required for her hooped skirt left little room for her three sons.

The styles of fashion might have changed over the years, but one's wealth and status were still displayed in their choice of attire.

Kathleen fingered the sprigged muslin of her white day dress, believing herself a fraud to be dressed in such finery. And yet based on the items in her rosewood box, whoever placed her on the vicar's doorstep had come from a place of means.

Had the woman who bore her ever worn such a gown? Had she a Season in London? What of her father? Had he been a gentleman of leisure or a merchant occupied with business?

The questions swirled the longer she lingered among her bene-factor's ancestors.

Who was she? Where did she belong?

One hand ventured from her waist to her neck and the small pendant she had strung on a fine gold chain.

A gift from her dear Reuben.

With him, she knew her identity.

Cherished friend. Beloved. Almost-betrothed.

The heart shape had been decorated with a forget-me-not among a strand of ivy. Symbols of love and fidelity.

Their promises spoken but vows unsaid.

She sighed.

More than a few miles separated them now.

A shout below stairs was followed by a multitude of footsteps across the hard floors. The earl must have arrived.

Kathleen picked up her skirts and hurried to join the staff as they prepared to welcome the master of the house. She reached the bottom of the grand staircase just as the door burst open and the earl strode inside.

In the instant it took for his vision to adjust to the dimmer light, she slowed her steps to a ladylike pace then dipped into a graceful curtsy. "My lord. Welcome back to Armstrong Park."

He widened his eyes at her greeting, then glanced around the entrance hall as if looking for her companion. However, the older woman was yet abed with a head cold and sniffles.

Kathleen knees trembled at the thought she was the acting lady of the house, but she willed a serene smile to her face as she observed the weary lines on the earl's face. His journey must have been both long and chilled. "Mrs. Pembroke is indisposed at present. However, may I order tea or a luncheon tray to be brought to the library for your refreshment?" She glanced at a footman who nodded. "I believe a fire has already been laid."

The earl removed his gloves and caped greatcoat, handing them to the butler. "Tea. And I'll expect your company as well."

"Yes, m'lord." She bobbed a quick curtsy and retreated toward the kitchens with as much poise as she could muster.

After a side trip to retrieve his belated gift, she reached the library moments after the tea cart was rolled through the entrance. She waved off the ever-present footman, and poured out in the same manner taught by her mother but reinforced by Mrs. Pembroke.

She set a cup and saucer before the earl. "How is your family, m'lord?"

"Well enough." He pushed aside a stack of paperwork with a slight frown and reached for the hot beverage. "When Jonathan and I left Rotherfield Park two days ago to deposit him back at Oxford on my way north, the countess and Simon were preparing their return to London."

Kathleen had studied the DeBrett's entry enough to identify both the younger son still at university and the eldest who was properly known as Viscount Lewisham, as befitting his father's heir.

"They should be well settled into the social whirl by the time we arrive."

Her stomach fluttered at the reminder as she placed the plate holding a sampling of finger sandwiches and cakes near the earl's elbow.

"And your celebration? Was it satisfactory?"

She blinked at his inquiry. "I made the most of the time with the staff and distributed the new liveries as is custom. I found it beneficial to stay busy in this first year without my father."

Lord Wiltshire's hand paused halfway to the plate of delicacies. "Forgive my oversight. I should have thought of you being alone and arranged for your journey sooner."

"Do not concern yourself. I was glad for the additional time here in the countryside. I was comforted with my memories even if an illness kept me from visiting friends in the village for Christmas."

He nodded as if understanding. "This region holds many memories for us both."

Kathleen thanked God for the conversational opening. "As he lay dying, my father mentioned your prior connection but I did not have time to question him. How did you know him?"

The earl leaned back in his chair, cradling his cup in his large hands. "Peter was my closest friend at university. I was not always in line for the earldom, you see. As a younger son, I thought to take holy orders, but my life didn't turn out how I'd planned and I questioned God's providence." A flash of grief dimmed his green eyes. "I set Peter up with a living here in my stead and somehow he became a symbol of the life I would never have. It was simpler to never look back than face the reminder of all I'd lost."

She sipped in silence, recalling all she'd heard from the servants. Other than immediately after her father's funeral, he had not visited the region in decades. Not even his best friend could bring him close. And yet... "I know that you wrote each other."

"Yes. But it was not the same friendship we once shared." He grimaced. "Peter always asked when I would return to the area so we could renew our acquaintance in person, but there were always business matters or the countess's societal expectations to fulfill and soon the years had slipped past."

She knew from the household gossip that the earl divided his time between London, his late mother's dower estate, or the estate acquired from his wife upon their marriage.

Sensing his regret, she sought for a lighter tone. "Was he always upstanding as a vicar should be or was he at all a—"

"Troublemaker?" The tilt to the earl's grin reminded her of Reuben's teasing nature. "I could tell you stories to sully his memory and reputation. But then he met Helena and, in an effort to win her hand, he put aside his mischief. I did not understand the transformation myself until I chanced to meet my Bella. Peter stood as witness to our marriage." The flash of joy that lit the earl's eyes was immediately clouded with grief as he drifted into memories only he recalled.

Meanwhile, Kathleen struggled to maintain her composure at the revelation. After all, the countess' given name was Phoebe, not Bella.

The details in her copy of DeBrett's had focused on the fact he had married the countess shortly after losing his father and that she delivered their first son a mere six months later. Kathleen's natural curiosity about those circumstances had been quickly swallowed by her trepidation over meeting the countess and her sons, including the heir who was close to her in age.

Since it would not do to have preconceived notions tainting their future acquaintance, she had focused her studies on the other families she was likely to meet in London.

However, on the fringes of her memory, it seemed there had been a brief mention of a first marriage to an unnamed woman...

She sipped her cooling tea and sought another subject change. "You mentioned your memories. Did you grow up here?"

"Yes." Lord Wiltshire shrugged away his melancholy mood. "I thank you for your descriptive letters detailing your excursions into the countryside. I used to enjoy that same vista overlooking the River Wharfe on my daily rides with my brother William."

"Whatever happened to him?"

"He was an officer on a naval ship. I would have liked to have heard more of his travels to exotic lands, but alas he perished after being cast adrift at the hands of mutineers." He frowned.

Yet another loss in the earl's life.

How did she keep stumbling into painful reminders? Perhaps it was better to end their conversation and return the cart to the kitchens.

As she began to assess her next action, her eyes fell upon her gift left abandoned beside the tea pot.

"Oh, I'd nearly forgotten." She set aside her empty cup, and soon delivered the package. "It is not much in light of your generosity toward me, but I thought you might like a token from Yorkshire. After all, we're known for the finest wool in all of England..."

He chuckled. "You certainly are a champion for my homeland." He untied the twine and unfolded the paper covering to reveal the black stockings inside. He laid a hand over them with a half-smile. "I had a similar pair in my youth..."

"I know they are handmade, but I asked the mother of a dear friend to assist. They are known in Armston for the quality of their woolen products and it was simple enough to contact them."

The earl raised an eyebrow. "The same source of the cloth for the garments my staff now model?"

"The same." She braced herself for a rebuke.

Instead, he rubbed a finger over the threads. "These seem like a more intimate use of thread than a purchase of finished cloth. Are you of such a connection to them? Is the enterprising weaver perhaps the same friend your father wrote of?"

"Without knowing the precise contents of that letter, I cannot confirm—"

"Your blush speaks for you." He set the stockings aside and folded his hands atop his waistcoat. "He wrote of a fatherless boy he had mentored for years. A boy who had grown into a young man of high character to be examined and considered. Is this the same man?"

"Yes." She fought to contain her smile and control her breathing.

Lord Wiltshire pinned her in a steady gaze. "And you have feelings for this man?"

"Very much so." She fingered the pendant on her chain.

He tapped a finger against his lips and made a humming sound.

She had to make him understand. "My father had given his personal blessing for our union, asking only that we wait to read the banns until he could consult with you. I assumed it was on the subject of a dowry of which I have no true expectation." The heat in her face was replaced with an unexpected welling of tears. "He was struck down in the road and gone within a week and our plans were delayed on account of mourning."

Lord Wiltshire set aside his empty cup. "I trust Peter's judgment regarding the young man's character. However, since we have already spent the time to prepare you for the Season and the countess is expecting us in a few days' time, we shall see it through. If you don't find another to turn your head among the ton, I will consider his suit..."

True joy bloomed in her chest. "Thank you, m'lord."

There could be no one else.

And now she was promised not only the experience of a lifetime with a London Season but the knowledge that Reuben waited at the end. With that incentive, surely she could survive whatever challenges society held.

With a lighter heart, she returned their used dishes to the cart and felt the earl's eyes on her.

"I am well pleased that Mrs. Pembroke's reports did not overstate your progress. And if my butler's uncharacteristic exuberance is to be believed, you are also responsible for the generosity shown at Twelfth Night. Is that where you spent the allotment I granted?"

"It is. Along with some of my own savings." With her practical needs already met, she had spent her allowance on behalf of others. That and on interesting books for herself. However, even with the expenses, she still had ample tucked into a corner of her wardrobe. Her smile wobbled. "Seeing their joy eased my loneliness this season."

His kind smile erased her worries. "That's something my Bella would have done. You have a kind heart. Do you take after your mother that way?"

"My mother died when I was but ten, but I would like to think she would be proud."

"As would your father, I am sure." With his refreshment concluded, the earl glanced around the library, then rose and crossed over to a stack of books and periodicals on a small table near the fireplace.

Kathleen held her breath as he examined her latest research.

"Weaving innovations. An interesting topic. Because of your friend?"

"And because it would be good for the village at large."

"Indeed."

She lifted her chin. "Indeed."

"Convince me." He claimed one of the chairs beside the fire.

She paced as she proceeded to lay out the arguments for modernization, the success of cotton mills, and the Addingham adaptations of similar machinery for wool. By centralizing the carders, spinners, weavers, and finishers under one roof, the consistent quality of the wool was maintained, more farmers had a market for their wool, and their output was only limited by the number of hours in the day. Machines would allow them to produce more in less time and therefore earn more profit.

"No more. You win." Earl held up his hands with a large grin and flashing green eyes that reminded her of Reuben whenever she had bested him during debates mediated by her father. "The idea has merit and I'll have my new steward look into such an investment. Perhaps a partnership with your friend?"

Her smile matched his for a moment, then dimmed. Oh, why had she so readily revealed her intelligence instead of maintaining a smokescreen of social expectations? What would Mrs. Pembroke say?

"I apologize. Without my mother's gentling presence, I fear my father encouraged active debate and invited me to learn alongside the boy he mentored."

"Peter always loved a strong debate and he taught you well. You must have inherited his sharp intellect."

Tears once again stung her eyes. When would the grieving end? "I know not whose intellect I inherited."

Lord Wiltshire blinked, then slowly nodded. "I remember now his reporting of the foundling on the vicarage steps. When was that again?"

"In the late summer of the year 1790. I was an infant of indeterminate age. The couple I consider my parents—Peter and Helena Harris who raised me—chose to celebrate my birthday on Midsummer's Eve."

The earl stretched out his legs as if settling into a deeper conversation. As if he truly cared. "Were there no clues to your parentage?"

She perched on the edge of a nearby chair and told him of the items in her box. "We assumed the letter must have contained all the necessary information, but regrettably, the rain that afternoon caused the ink to run."

"I've always enjoyed a good mystery. Would you allow me a look?"

It seemed peculiar to open herself to the man's scrutiny, but she'd seen glimpses of her father's friend in their conversation and a connection of sorts was forming between them. If he had the means to find the answers she'd wished for, she could not miss the opportunity.

She nodded.

He rang for a servant to clear the tray and sent someone to her room to fetch the box.

A few minutes later, Kathleen had secured her packet of letters in her lap while the earl examined the other contents.

"I never had my same initials on a handkerchief but knew some in my set who did. I think I've seen this monogram before somewhere, but will have to think more on the matter. The silk is of a superior quality and the christening gown has the appearance of similar wealth." He set those items aside and carefully unfolded the paper, holding it to the light. "These smeared lines would not be a bill of sale or an invitation to a dance since they were deliberately left with a babe."

He frowned slightly as if lost in thought. "It could be a certificate of birth or even marriage lines to prove the legitimacy of the child. Although that does not explain why you were not given to a distant family member. Unless that was the purpose of the writing on the outside of the note..."

His conclusions were nothing she hadn't speculated about herself.

"Do you mind if I keep this and have my solicitor in London look into the matter?"

Momentary alarm gave way to peace for the earl's connections extended far beyond those of an Armston vicar. "You may."

"I will see to it." Lord Wiltshire rose and crossed back to his desk with the paper in hand. "Now, while I have enjoyed our conversation and the Yorkshire welcome, I should acquaint myself with the ledgers before dinner." He glanced over his shoulder with a slight smile. "I must be prepared when quizzing my new steward on the morrow."

Heat rose in her face as she replaced her treasures into her box, curtsied, and made her exit.

However, as she ascended the stairs, she embraced hope.

Upon closer acquaintance, the earl was not as stiff or formal as she'd once assumed. With him as an ally, she was actually looking forward to her time in London.

Chapter Six

January, Armston

S aturday morning, Reuben paused to catch his breath inside the warm and brightly lit shop. He was not the only laborer, for most of the stations were occupied.

If only Kathleen could see the changes.

Her latest note had conveyed her hope to entice the earl into a tour of the countryside and village after his arrival. A tour where she had hoped to introduce them.

While he felt unprepared for such an encounter, what sort of a man did it make him to be afraid to face an earl with the prize of Kathleen at stake?

He tucked his shirt more firmly into the waistband of his trousers. For a moment, he regretted not wearing his Sunday best in anticipation of such an introduction, but that constricting attire was unsuited for the work still to be done. Especially when that included moving bundles of wool to the carding station.

Halfway through the task, he caught a glimpse of movement through the tall windows. A carriage bearing the earl's crest on the door came to a stop outside the double doors and he detoured to investigate.

Except Mr. Radcliff was the only occupant and Reuben swallowed his disappointment.

With the rents already paid in full, what business could the earl's steward have with him?

"Good day, sir." Reuben nodded his head in greeting as the man stepped down from the carriage.

"And to you, Mr. Cooke." The steward looked past him to the building. "Could I impose upon you for a tour of the enterprise within these doors?"

"It would be no imposition." Reuben gestured for the visitor to proceed inside.

Why come now? Unless there was a question of property valuation to levy a higher rent than the exorbitant fee the previous steward had extracted.

Nay. Better to withhold judgment in favor of an amiable working relationship.

Once indoors, Reuben led the man past the carding and spinning stations, ignoring the speculative glances from the village women processing the fibers into spools of thread.

"Are any of these specifically for carpets?" Mr. Radcliff peered closely at the pile of raw wool.

"A knowledgeable question." Reuben waved for the women to continue their work. "Is Armstrong Park in need of another supply?"

The steward shrugged. "I was merely curious and attempting to educate myself in the processes."

In light of the man's curiosity, Reuben expanded his explanations of the process as they meandered on past the dying station toward the looms where various types of cloth were being woven.

His mother never paused the motion of the pedals and shuttle, but he caught her frown. He understood her hesitation. The previous steward's behavior had left many of the villagers suspicious of the new one's motives, but in their few interactions, Reuben had found him a decent fellow.

"This weave appears similar to our last purchase."

"It is." Reuben smiled. "In fact, when complete, this piece will be part of the next order. Does it meet with your satisfaction?"

The man nodded. "It does."

Reuben strolled on to complete the tour in the finishing and storage sections of the building where the relative quiet made it easier to converse. "Do you have any questions?"

"What is your goal for this enterprise?"

Reuben folded his hands behind his back. "We used to be scattered among various households, but having everyone under one roof has simplified things and revealed opportunities for growth. I have approached several additional farmers to secure their cooperation and we should have an ample supply of wool in a few months' time." He waved a hand at the nearly empty shelves around them. "The finished goods not designated for Armstrong Park are transported to Addingham and sold there to merchants who in turn journey on to Leeds."

"I am familiar with the bustling markets of Leeds. Woolen goods are the mainstay of their commerce."

Reuben frowned. "I fear I did not receive as high a price as our cloth demands, but there is a challenge in competing with the mills and workhouses in Addingham while the merchant is also eager to make a profit. However, this current situation is a step in the right direction. Someday I hope to—" He cut himself short and his face heated. "Forgive me. I get carried away with the possibilities."

Mr. Radcliff smiled with a knowing gleam in his eyes. "Go on. I'm intrigued."

Reuben drew in a deep breath. "Someday I hope to put enough aside to repair the water wheel." He waved at the wall closest the river and the idle remains of the building's former use as a grain mill. "I have been studying mechanized machinery and hope to invest in a powered loom or spinning machine. Once operational, it would naturally increase the output from each individual weaver. Not only would we be able to easily fulfill Armstrong Park's annual needs, but could also pursue additional contracts with regional estates to avoid the competition of the overcrowded Addingham markets."

"A matter of supply and demand. Not to mention that like our ongoing arrangement, eliminating the merchant's fee increases your profit while saving the estates equal measure. It is a sound business practice indeed and I have no doubt His Lordship would approve, for we spoke of it yesterday."

Even if the earl was not present to deliver the praise, Reuben soaked in the implied commendation.

The steward narrowed his eyes. "Have you calculated the expense of the repairs and machinery in question? How much time would be required to purchase and install such equipment? Have you given thought to the training of the workers on their operation? To avoiding the Luddite issues that erupted in Leeds last year?"

They were questions he had investigated privately if only to temper his rising ambitions fueled by a desire to provide a future for Kathleen.

He glanced at his mother whose raised eyebrows signaled her obvious eavesdropping, but then she nodded her approval.

Except the depth of questions revealed the steward was not as uneducated as he'd given him reason to believe earlier.

Reuben folded his arms. "How come you to know so much about our woolen industry?"

"I was raised in Norfolk." Mr. Radcliff cleared his throat. "However, I readily admit a speedy education yesterday from the earl and the articulate Miss Harris."

"Ah." Kathleen. Of course. And the earl? "Where are they now?"

"Off to London this morn in a caravan of carriages. I do not expect to see them until June at least."

Disappointment clawed at his heart even though the increasing distance had been expected. If only her plans for a country drive had come to fruition, he might have seen her once more before her departure.

"In their absence, I have been given a directive that will require your cooperation. I am to educate myself on the subject of mechanized weaving operations such as you have described and then have the written authorization to forge a partnership with you should the terms meet with your satisfaction."

Reuben felt breathless as tingles spread through his body. "What would such a partnership entail?"

"Shall we remove ourselves to the public house to discuss the particulars?"

Over the next half hour, Mr. Radcliff laid out the details of the proposed arrangement whereby Reuben would be given the necessary funds to immediately repair the water wheel and outfit the workshop with machinery. In exchange, they dickered over what percentage of the resulting profits would be used to repay the initial investment. However, once that loan was repaid, the profits could then be re-invested into a steam experiment. Or a secondary loan could be arranged at that stage if deemed wise. In the meantime, the venture would be officially named the Armston Weaving Cooperative.

Reuben drew a deep breath. "The arrangement sounds more than fair and in fact generous. However, I need to clarify that my past purpose in consolidating several cottage enterprises and sharing the profits was not to build a name for myself. Therefore, with any future expansion, I would not wish to subdue the village competition, but rather to create a business to benefit the region."

"Miss Harris implied the same." Mr. Radcliff raised an eyebrow as if confused a woman could have such insight.

"She and I have discussed such possibilities at her father's table over the past few years and more recently by letter."

The steward nodded, but a curious gleam crept into his eyes as if just now realizing the depth of their connection. No doubt a few well-placed questions around town would fill in the gaps of knowledge regarding Reuben's intentions for the vicar's lovely daughter.

Reuben straightened his shoulders. "What is the next step before we officially launch this venture?"

"I have drawn up a contract containing the terms I first proposed." Mr. Radcliff stood and gestured toward the door. "Either of us can make an addendum with the changes we discussed."

Reuben followed him outside and back toward the workshop. "I would like some time to ponder the ramifications before signing." As well as time to consult his mother. And pray.

"Understandable." Mr. Radcliff did not seem irritated by the delay. "I will use the time to acquaint myself further with the reading material Miss Harris left behind."

Reuben laughed. "I suspect she has already given me the same titles."

"Likely." The steward reached into the carriage for a leather pouch, and then withdrew a sheet of parchment. "If you are agreeable, should I expect you Monday morning to discuss the final terms and affix our signatures?"

"You may."

"One more thing..." The steward shifted on his feet. "Miss Harris requested that I allow the exchange of your personal letters through the packet containing my weekly report to Lord Wiltshire. It goes out in Monday's post."

Reuben accepted the contract and the offer with a slight nod.

The charity of the arrangement left a sour taste in his mouth, but with an unreliable postal service that charged by both the page and the distance, he was sensible enough to accept the generous offer in order to maintain their communication. Otherwise his profits would be spent paying postage instead of saving for their future.

With their business concluded, Reuben bid the man farewell and soon the carriage rolled away toward Armstrong Park.

Leaving Reuben alone outside the old mill building with churning emotions.

His dear Kathleen.

Had she instigated more than their exchange of letters? Had the weaving cooperative also been orchestrated by her hand?

His heart swelled with gratitude, and yet he felt small beside her increasing influence. Unworthy of her attention or affection.

No. He would simply have to prove her faith in his abilities no matter the additional work it would require.

He turned for the door, his mind already spinning with hope-filled ideas for the future, both for them and the village at large. However, despite the unsigned contract in his hand, his shoulders already carried the weight of the earl's trust and financial investment.

He could not fail Lord Wiltshire.

He could not fail Kathleen.

And he certainly could not let the current opportunity come to naught else he be unprepared to ask the earl for her hand in June.

Mid-January

Kathleen returned her quill to the ink stand on her writing desk, then rotated her wrist several times to release the soreness.

She glanced at the stack of papers recounting the last few days with a smile. Reuben had asked her to tell him everything. And yet there were not words enough to describe her time thus far in London.

If she'd thought the move from Armston to the earl's estate on the hill overwhelming, arriving in the crowded city in the center of the social swirl was worse.

Mrs. Pembroke might have taught her the proper words to say, but nothing could have prepared her for the constant noise, the stench that lingered in the air, and the late hours.

She stifled a yawn. Only the servants—and those accustomed to country life—arose with the dawn.

Hooves clattered on the cobblestone street outside the window of her bedchamber on the third floor of the earl's townhouse and somewhere a delivery man shouted a greeting. The sounds of a city at midday were an unspoken reminder that it would not be long before her schedule would be dictated by the countess.

She picked up the quill and resumed writing.

I pray you forgive my ramblings but there you have it. The full account of my journey with the earl from Yorkshire to London, my superficial education about his numerous holdings, the treasured conversations recalling his memories of my father during their school days, my first glimpse of London, my introduction to his family, and finally my terrifying debut at Almack's last night.

Assuming I made a favorable impression upon the gentle ladies of the ton, today I might begin to receive invitations in my own right to concerts and balls. Otherwise, I shall be content to trail along behind Lady Wiltshire to her engagements. Lord Wiltshire is often occupied with government and estate matters and has yet to make an appearance at such things.

In the meantime, it is my understanding that our days will be spent calling on friends, taking a ride in Hyde Park to be seen, or lingering at home to receive callers. Evenings are otherwise engaged with dinner parties, concerts, and balls that last until the wee hours of the morning. With nary a free moment to simply read or a quiet moment to contemplate the deeper things.

I sincerely wish you were by my side to experience all of this for yourself. However, I vow to embrace every moment and to share it all with you either by letter or upon my return to my beloved Yorkshire.

For now, I will conclude this letter and give it to a footman to include with the weekly post. Did Mr. Radcliff speak with you?...

A moment later, she signed her name to the missive and replaced the quill in the ink stand.

After rising from the straight-backed wooden chair, she worked the knots from her neck and sore back. The blisters on her feet from all the dancing plus the ache of other unused muscles shrieked their complaints.

She paced the thick carpet. While smaller than her lodgings at Armstrong Park, the room was just as lavishly decorated.

Beautiful, but it did not feel like home.

Or any home at all, especially after observing the tension among the staff when dealing with their mistress. Not to mention the undercurrent of suppressed animosity between the earl and his wife.

In her descriptions for Reuben, she had glossed over her initial meeting with Lady Wiltshire. From the moment the earl had led her into the drawing room and introduced her to the elegantly dressed blonde seated on the damask settee, it was readily apparent that championing the orphaned daughter of an old friend was a decision the earl had foisted upon his lady wife.

The woman's shrewd gaze had immediately focused on Kathleen's hair and her lips tightened before she turned icy blue eyes to her husband and then to the portrait of their family hanging above the fireplace.

The portrait displaying a blonde woman, her red-haired husband, and their sons. One with light brown hair and the other with reddish-blond hair.

A similar shade to Kathleen's.

A moment later, Lady Wiltshire had assumed her role as hostess and rang for tea. Over the refreshment, the countess politely inquired of Kathleen's training, carelessly dismissed Mrs. Pembroke to find a new debutante to advise, and reluctantly agreed to call in a favor to secure an invitation to Almack's.

It was all quite proper, but Kathleen could not forget the woman's cold eyes as she observed Lord Wiltshire's kindly behavior toward his ward.

It had been the last time she had seen the earl since their arrival.

Aside from Parliamentary duties involving wars both in the Americas and on the Continent, his time was occupied with running at least three estates plus additional lucrative business ventures.

Her eyes widened.

The earl might be sequestered in the library even now. And if she were to slip downstairs to select a book to read in the walled garden behind the townhouse, she might have a moment for a brief conversation with her only friend in London.

Her plan made, she quickly sealed and addressed Reuben's letter, intending to add it to the packet personally.

However, before she could escape her room, there was a knock on the door. She opened the portal to find her lady's maid.

"The countess has requested you attend her in the drawing room during her hours at home. I'm to help you into proper dress."

Dread swirled in her midsection. Would she be invited into the conversations or expected to sit silently as mere evidence of the

Wiltshires' generosity toward those less fortunate? She'd already tasted that treatment last evening at Almack's.

Kathleen sighed. "I thank you for your assistance, but first I have a quick errand—"

"Oh." The maid glanced at the letter and tried to tug it from Kathleen's hand. "I'll see to that for you."

"Lord Wiltshire gave his permission to have it franked for Yorkshire." The noble seal assured free but speedy delivery.

The maid lifted an eyebrow as if questioning the truthfulness of her claim, but Kathleen held her gaze until the servant remembered her position and relented. And summoned a footman to see to the task instead.

With her quest to accidentally encounter the earl thwarted, Kathleen submitted to the girl's ministrations.

While being laced into tighter stays and wrapped in a different gown, she endured the maid's prattling on about Viscount Lewisham being expected to call and stay for dinner before escorting his mother and Kathleen to a ball that evening. While the idea of a ball ignited her curiosity, she tuned out the chatter about gowns.

By the time the maid deemed her hair suitably arranged, Kathleen was past the appointed hour as she descended the stairs and turned into the drawing room.

Lady Wiltshire was settled in her favorite spot on the settee with her skirts prettily arranged about her ankles as she conversed with two other equally elegant women. She looked up at Kathleen's arrival with a sickly sweet smile. "Ah, you've come at last. Be a dear and see what is keeping our tea."

Kathleen nodded and retreated on the errand. A servant's task and yet any excuse to delay the inevitable slights was welcomed.

Too soon, she was back in their company and instructed to pour the tea. Another task to keep her hands busy and delay the introductions.

Kathleen was in the process of serving the countess when a tall man about her age entered without escort of the butler. Lady Wiltshire waved the cup aside, then extended her hands to the newcomer. "Lewisham. You've arrived at last."

The man strode to his mother's side and submitted to her fawning—and that of their guests—as if it were his due while Kathleen continued to serve.

"Such a handsome son. You must be so proud."

"Indeed. He reminds me of his father at that age."

"Have any of the lovely young ladies in town caught your eye?"

The viscount gave a sharp tug on his waistcoat before taking a seat near his mother. "I do not believe I am ready to be caught. With a title and promise of a fortune, I am free to partake of pleasures for a season, do you not think?" He tilted his head with a slight smile as if making a jest.

The other women tittered but Kathleen was not amused.

According to the servants' gossip, he maintained a separate household in town in addition to an inherited estate, but was more often found in the company of other reckless young men over a hand of cards at a gentleman's club when not dancing late into the night.

Once everyone was served, Kathleen poured herself a cup of tea and unable to delay the inevitable any longer, she claimed a cushioned chair near the others.

The woman to Lady Wiltshire's right stiffened as if surprised at Kathleen's familiarity, but their charming hostess quickly made the proper introductions.

But while the others had titles, she was simply Miss Harris. Lord Wiltshire's charitable duty for the Season.

The ladies returned to their conversation without a second look, but Lewisham sneered as his gaze ran from her hair to her shoes. As if she were a piece of dung under his boot. An unnecessary expense depriving his mother of a new gown.

Remember who you are.

The echo of her father's words had been reinforced by the earl's kindness. Unless he had also been seeing her as an entertaining diversion from his regular duties.

Before she could acknowledge the sting of that thought, the butler announced the arrival of Lady Montgomery and her daughter Miss Joanna Montgomery.

Lady Wiltshire rose to greet the newcomers and made the necessary introductions before seating them in places of honor. She then gestured for Kathleen to serve, all while expressing her sympathy for Lord Townshend's failing health.

Apparently, if the other whispers in the room were to be believed, the lady's father-in-law was not expected to survive the illness and she would be a marchioness before the year was out.

Which explained Lady Wiltshire's fawning behavior toward one with higher prospects and connections.

From her position on the fringes, Kathleen observed the younger woman casting side-glances at Lord Lewisham.

According to Mrs. Pembroke's lessons, suitable matches were advanced during social calls as often as at balls...and it appeared Miss Montgomery or her mother had their own scheme in mind.

After a few minutes of polite conversation, Lady Wiltshire conveniently divulged that her son was dining with them later before escorting his dear mother to Howard's Ball that evening.

Lady Montgomery tilted her head toward Kathleen. "And will your...ward...be accompanying you?"

If Kathleen hadn't been watching, she would have missed the countess' moment of panic followed by her serene smile.

"Of course. Lord Wiltshire has made it his mission to give her a season in fulfillment of a promise to an old friend and since she gained the Almack's approval last night, I will be doing my part in the endeavor."

Miss Montgomery's eyes gleamed. "If I may be so bold, since we will also be at Howard's this evening, perhaps I can impose upon a cousin, Baron Tattershall, to accompany Miss Harris."

As if one favor—pairing the poor orphan with a suitable prospect—would assure the opportunity of a second encounter with her matrimonial prey and win the support of his mother.

The countess agreed with a subdued but equally delighted nod before shifting the conversation toward other rumored attendees.

Kathleen had scarcely set aside her empty tea cup in favor of her embroidery when Miss Montgomery persuaded her to take a turn about the room as if to make a further acquaintance. However, the subsequent whispered conversation was monopolized by the young woman's touting of her own achievements and a request to put in a good word with the viscount.

As if Kathleen held any sway in that regard.

Then Miss Montgomery's laughter suddenly pealed across the room, attracting the attention of the same object of her desire.

Confirming that Kathleen's presence was a mere prop in a grander scheme.

Then again, being used in such a manner could not be worse than being overlooked completely. Or disparaged.

God only knew if Miss Montgomery might become a friend to help pass her months in London.

Chapter Seven

Late January

Reuben sank onto the cushioned chair beside the fire in their reclaimed front room and unfolded Kathleen's extremely thick letter. It had been delivered to the weaving cooperative building earlier in the day by a servant from Armstrong Park but since he'd been occupied overseeing the workmen on the water wheel, he'd saved it as a reward.

He tilted the pages toward the flickering light and savored the love-filled words that opened her missive.

He glanced at the other chair nearby. How often had he imagined her sitting there with him of an evening? Sharing the quiet moments in reflection and companionship before retiring to their bedchamber?

His face heated at the direction of his thoughts.

"If it is not too personal of a nature, I would enjoy hearing what she has to say." His mother claimed Kathleen's chair and tugged her basket of mending closer.

"Of course." He cleared his throat, omitted the opening greetings and the emotions they evoked, then began to read aloud Kathleen's descriptions of the journey to London and the variety of countryside they'd driven through. Since he had never ventured further than the twenty miles to Leeds in his lifetime—and that only a few times—her words stirred a longing to make his own journey in the future.

She wrote further of how she'd enjoyed their time near Oxford where her father had spent so much time as a student and how they had stayed overnight in Wheatley instead of merely exchanging the horses for a fresh set.

"My family once had such an establishment that saw to the needs of travelers." A plaintive tone shaded his mother's words.

"You've told me the stories of your childhood but never the true location." Why had the lack of information only just now occurred to him?

She waved a hand dismissively and focused again on her stitching. "The inn and my family are both gone now. Sometimes the past is best left to rest."

Perhaps. But the roused questions now occupied a portion of his mind.

"Go on now." She pointed to the pages. "What else does she say?"

He turned his attention to the continuing saga and voiced her first impressions of London. In essence, it was large, crowded, loud, and rank-smelling.

He smirked. "It appears Kathleen is still a country girl at heart." The same simple girl he'd fallen in love with.

His mother smiled. "It will be good for her to remember her roots in the coming weeks."

Kathleen's clear penmanship continued with a description of the intricate architectural details, wrought iron railings, and carved stonework on the buildings. Of the rows of multi-storied townhomes set along cobbled streets with the carriage houses and kitchen gardens tucked away behind each.

The tone shifted slightly when she recounted her initial meeting with Lady Wiltshire in the elaborately decorated drawing room. While she never alluded to her feelings directly, he knew her well enough to recognize that she had come away from the encounter insecure and in doubt of her worth.

If only he were there to encourage her.

And yet he would feel equally out of place in such a situation.

At a sniff nearby, he glanced up to find his mother's face twisted with a pained expression in sympathy.

He prayed the countess would come to see Kathleen's heart and value.

Pushing aside his concern, he continued on with her descriptions of her official debut into society at a place called Almack's.

His mother leaned forward and closed her eyes as if imagining herself there. Was it a part of the feminine nature to long for romance like a princess?

Kathleen's depiction of the scene and evening events unfurled with a description of the ballroom, the white-gowned debutantes, the company of chaperones and sponsors around the perimeter, and the abundance of fancy-dressed dandies with cravats so tight their noses were in the air. She detailed the multitude of fabrics and even the intricate details of waistcoats observed up close during the dances.

As he turned the pages spurred on by his mother's rapt attention, he relayed Kathleen's fears that she would be a wallflower on a chair in the corner but also her relief that the mere name of Lord and Lady Wiltshire had assured her a few names on her dance card. Those partners had introduced her to others and so on until her feet were sore and she rarely saw a chair at all between sips of lukewarm punch.

He paused his reading to imagine her in such a setting.

His beautiful Kathleen with the candlelight setting her reddish blonde hair aglow and the flash of her smile behind pink lips. The feel of her hand in his. The swish of her skirts against his trousers as they danced.

Not for the first time, he acknowledged his jealousy of an unnamed gentleman with an intricate cravat and embroidered waistcoat who had the right to spend time with his beloved.

He cast a brief look at his dirty work shirt and trousers.

However, due to the earl's offer of a financial partnership and given enough time, he might eventually have a local standing as that of a merchant.

But even were he to dramatically improve his position, it would not be enough to compare with the parade of faceless men who would entertain and distract his dear Kathleen at her next event.

"It is a different world, son." His mother's voice conveyed a depth of insight into his musings.

"I know. A world I don't belong to." Yet one he longed for.

She frowned. "Guard your heart with the knowledge that foremost you are a child of God."

"I know this to be true. But while I am assured of an eternal inheritance, what of the temporal?"

"What of it?"

"Not long ago I was a mere tenant farmer and weaver struggling with your assistance to turn my flock of sheep into enough cloth to provide for our needs and someday support a wife and family. Even with the new opportunities before me, the villagers still view me the poor fatherless boy not worthy to win the hand of the vicar's daughter." He skimmed a hand through his hair, then down his face. "Now she is even further out of reach and I cannot help but wish..."

A sigh echoed his emotions. "I know all too well what it is like to wish things were different. To see another's position and imagine our roles were reversed."

"What role do you desire?" The nagging doubts of his child-hood returned. "That of a wife in addition to being a weaver? Because if you desire a husband—"

"Nay." Her harsh voice rejected the idea. "I made a vow and my loyalty lies with my first love."

In the heavy silence that followed, he wrestled with the urge as a man to demand answers while as a son respecting her privacy and the years of sacrifice on his behalf.

If he was illegitimate, was it better not to know the truth? Or would a delayed revelation only pull Kathleen into the repercussions?

He swallowed hard, then broached the topic. "Why do you never speak of my father?"

"There is only grief in that subject." Again, he caught a glimpse of the pain he'd often seen in her eyes.

The pain of a broken heart put there by the father he never knew. Reuben clenched his jaw.

His mother thrust her emotions behind a wall of determination and narrowed her eyes. "Know this, that the lack of a father's daily influence does not alter the man you have become under the vicar's oversight. Stand firm on that character."

A portion of the ache in his chest eased at the reminder of Vicar Harris and their lessons.

His mother put aside her mending and stood. "You have all the foundation you need. Now remain true to yourself and build on it."

With those parting words, she retreated to her bedchamber.

In the quiet, he returned his attention to the remainder of Kathleen's letter where it seemed she would be quite occupied with activity in the weeks and months to come.

There was comfort in knowing she had remembered him and asked after his contract with the steward. And for the moment, promised a return to the region.

A return to him.

However, his frustrations over their separation jumbled with his unanswered questions, churning in his mind and foretelling a restless night.

But what could he do?

Nothing.

Except pray.

And channel his emotions into the weaving cooperative's improvements.

And use his letters to keep Kathleen connected to her roots. To challenge her to remain true to herself.

If only he could remember the same.

Mid-March

Kathleen skirted the crush of dancers in the ballroom and edged toward the refreshment table for a cup of punch.

It was yet relatively early in the evening and if the precedent held, it would be hours before Lady Wiltshire called for the carriage.

Tonight's event was just another in a long string of engagements that had unfurled since the Howard's Ball. Each one was much like the last and she was still meeting new people and pairing faces to the dry stories inside her now well-worn copy of DeBrett's Peerage.

After a few sips, she searched out an empty chair along the wall. However, she had been recently on the dance floor for three consecutive sets, unlike many of the quiet girls seated nearby.

Unlike the village assemblies of her youth.

She recalled Reuben's first letter to London from almost two months ago. It still haunted her with the challenge to stay connected to her roots and be herself.

If only she knew who that was.

Orphaned child of Vicar Harris? Assumed ward of a country earl? Bluestocking because of her interest in science and learning? Debutante presumed to be in search of a husband? Or a pawn in Lady Wiltshire's quest to forward a favorable match on behalf of her firstborn?

While the countess claimed the credit for their invitations, Kathleen believed the rising popularity was more the result of their peripheral association with the Montgomerys, especially Miss Montgomery who had been seen more and more often near Lewisham even if he was not the only gentleman to have won her attentions.

And the young lady seemed to attach herself to Kathleen's side at whim...only to abandon her.

If only Reuben were here to advise her on how to behave.

Then again, he knew where he belonged. She was the one without roots. But based on the bits of fabric in her rosewood box, there was wealth somewhere in her background. If circumstances had been different, she might have grown up in this world after all.

She lifted her chin, determined to enjoy herself with what time she had remaining in London.

After relinquishing her punch cup to a servant, she immersed herself in the swirling colors under the light of the chandeliers and breathed in the exotic perfumes. Nowhere else had she felt so much like a princess from one of Charles Perrault's fairy tales.

What could she tell Reuben that she had not already described?

Her letters of late sounded like more of the same, especially when it came to fashion and her latest gown. Or betrothal announcements among people she herself had scarcely met while his only connection was through her letters.

While his responses spoke of water wheels, machinery, and sheep.

Perhaps she should eavesdrop on the men's conversations and pick up a political morsel to share instead? After all, his birthday was less than a week away.

She cast her gaze about the room and noticed an alcove near the card tables where the husbands and fathers mingled. It would be perfect for her purpose.

Halfway to her destination, she was halted by Miss Montgomery's hand on her arm and whisper in her ear. "Did you see her? I cannot believe she dared show her face."

"Who?" And why?

Miss Montgomery linked arms with Kathleen and made a show of walking the perimeter together as she whispered in Kathleen's ear the latest gossip. Cutting and derisive, but equally informative. Except instead of news about a debutante's prospects or a gentleman's fortune, this time there was true scandal.

A certain Miss Fletcher had taken the previous Season by storm, catching the attention of numerous gentlemen. Rumor had it there had been a dozen offers for her hand and at least one duel between potential suitors.

Kathleen noticed the mixture of awe and jealousy in her companion's voice. "What happened then?"

"Midway through the Season, she suddenly quit for the countryside." Miss Montgomery cast a quick glance around. "I heard her father sent her to live with a distant relative because..." She lowered her voice even further. "She was enlarging without benefit of marriage."

Kathleen gasped. She had seen the blatant flirtations of many and heard the warnings that such behavior could lead to ruin. But to be with child as a result?

"Scandalous, I know. She should have rushed into marriage where she could find it to rectify her mistake." Miss Montgomery affected a delicious shiver. "Your Lady Wiltshire is not the first to have done so."

Kathleen blinked in shock at the undisguised reference to something she herself had only speculated about based on De-Brett's dates and simple mental mathematics.

If indeed there had been early affection between the earl and his wife to warrant such haste, it had waned years ago. For like most of the ton—if the servants' gossip was to be believed—the earl and countess maintained separate bedchambers.

"And now to return to proper society as though nothing ever happened?" Miss Montgomery preened as they passed by a cluster of young gentlemen.

Kathleen reeled, feeling as though someone needed to defend the girl from the gossip. "Perhaps nothing did."

Miss Montgomery dismissed the notion with a shake of her pretty head. "Her family should have made her excuses rather than have her simply disappear. Not only that, I believe she has put on weight and she seems more subdued than before." She gestured across the room to a young woman standing beside an older man, likely her father.

Kathleen could see the woman's struggle to ignore the whispers around her as the mothers of the ton pulled their daughters aside and also pointed. Likely using the girl as a warning.

And yet there was something in the woman's demeanor that spoke of innocence. As if she were the injured party.

Kathleen frowned. "Why would she return so publicly?" Especially if the rogue who abandoned her in such a condition was also circulating among the ton?

Miss Montgomery scoffed as they completed their turn about the ballroom. "Her father likely hopes for another attempt at fetching her a husband. Mark my words. She'll marry a lecherous twice-widowed old man who will overlook her past improprieties in hopes of securing an heir."

Bile rose in her throat to realize that without the earl's support and his implied promise to consider Reuben's suit in a few short months, such might be her own fate.

"If what you say is true, what has become of the child?"

Miss Montgomery wrinkled her nose. "If the babe survived, it will probably be raised by tenants so happy to have a child they can overlook a matter of parentage."

With that declaration, she darted off to dissect the gossip with another willing ear. Meanwhile, Kathleen found a nearby chair and sank onto its support.

A childless couple overlooking a matter of parentage? If it wasn't for Peter and Helena Harris being in such a situation themselves, Kathleen might have been raised in an orphanage until she was of age to be apprenticed to a merchant.

Thank heavens Lady Wiltshire either did not know of or chose to ignore such information about Kathleen's heritage or else Kathleen might have been observed with the same biting speculation directed at the poor Miss Fletcher.

A chill settled over her shoulders at the thought.

Was it possible that her own mother had been a part of this world and had to flee a similar scandal? Had the woman returned to her family with empty arms and sought a different future?

The swirl of dancers continued before her.

Could she in fact have crossed paths with her mother over the past weeks of activity? Would she ever know?

The unanswered questions tormented her.

Seeking a distraction, she resolved to complete her original quest and find an interesting bit of information or topic to share with Reuben.

She made her way toward the unoccupied alcove and stood near the wall as if watching the dancers. Behind her there was a distinct rumble of male voices but the words were overshadowed by the music and general noise of the crowded ballroom.

She slipped a bit further to her right behind a decorative drape of fabric that served to muffle the ballroom sounds in favor of the other conversation. Feigning a bland expression, she focused on their words.

They debated over sending additional soldiers to either the conflict in America to prevent their trade with Napoleon's France or to Wellington in the Iberian Peninsula to assist in the liberation of Spain. The naysayers worried only about the expense and the impact of higher taxation on the common man.

Oh, to be welcomed to such a discussion.

While inwardly composing her letter to Reuben, she caught snippets of a different conversation. Something about a horse race and a stallion breeding.

Heat flooded her neck and she began her retreat.

However, after two steps in the direction of the punch bowl, a man stepped in front of her, blocking her escape. She looked up from his straining waistcoat to his flushed face.

Miss Montgomery's cousin, the Baron Tattersall.

"Clever girl finding a way for us to have a private moment."

"Nay. I was not here for you—"

His eyes narrowed. "There is another seeking your attentions?" His gaze dipped to the flesh exposed above her bodice like it had during every previous meeting and uncomfortable dance. "Surely I can convince you otherwise."

"Nay. Pray excuse me, sir, but I see your cousin." Her skin prickled with caution and the desire to flee.

"Indeed." A raised eyebrow exposed her falsehood since his body obstructed her view completely.

She could see no one.

And therefore no one could see her.

Her heart beat rapidly in her chest.

"I see I shall have to impose upon my relative to assure your future favors next time we so meet." The baron snatched her hand, slowly raising it to his lips. "And I assure you heartily, there will be a next time."

After an excruciating moment, he released her and stepped to the side, allowing her rushed escape with a low chuckle.

For the remainder of the evening, she stayed close to Miss Montgomery or Lady Wiltshire when not occupied quite visibly on the dance floor or in the company of respectable matrons.

All the while, her heart longed for Reuben and clung to the memory of the last time she'd seen him.

The day he had kissed her hand outside the vicarage and helped her into the earl's carriage.

Godspeed in your journey, Miss Harris.

Oh, that her journey would bring her back to him.

Chapter Eight

Mid-March

R euben strode away from the public house with two squares of fabric tucked away in his coat pockets and a smile on his face.

One was cloth from the Armston Weaving Cooperative's newly operational water-powered loom that he had used to demonstrate the consistent quality they could deliver.

The other was a color sample from the livery of an estate to their northwest. Assuming Reuben's workers could match the dye and the resulting thread was approved by the steward, it would be his third recurring contract including the order from Armstrong Park.

Mr. Radcliff would likely be surprised when Reuben delivered his first loan payment at the end of the month.

There was a benefit from turning his emotional turmoil into action.

And while he was trying not to calculate the date of Kathleen's possible return too soon, he was already composing a letter to share the progress with her.

"Ho there, Mr. Cooke."

Reuben turned back as the butcher hurried across the muddy street.

"The earl's housekeeper was just here and asked me to deliver a letter for you." The man waved a folded packet in his beefy hand and waggled his eyebrows. "From London."

"Thank you." Reuben met the man halfway and accepted the letter with a quick head bob that sufficed for manners in the village.

The action was probably far from proper in Kathleen's circles nowadays, but how was one to know if one shopkeeper ranked above a fellow merchant? Or if as a younger man he should defer to his elders?

At any rate, the man nodded in return, then hastened back to his establishment.

Leaving Reuben alone in the middle of the street with another treasure. And it had arrived on his birthday no less.

Not wanting to wait to read it but also desiring privacy, he slipped around the corner of the old mill building and seated himself on a rock beside the slowly rotating wheel before breaking the seal.

He smiled at Kathleen's stated purpose that in honor of his birthday, she was deliberately avoiding a description of yet another ball gown and instead relaying something of more interest to men.

He read on with interest as she revealed the bit of information she'd learned about war. If only he was there to debate the strategies in play.

You will never believe the lengths I had to go to in order to glean this information. I fear my position near the drapery invited the wrong impression but I soon made my escape.

Escape? Had she been in danger with him half a country away?

Suddenly he had half a mind to write to the earl and request an increased watch over Kathleen's safety.

I am baffled to fathom why Baron Tattersall would have any interest in me other than the amusement of a conquest. I have no anticipation of wealth or position to attract his attention.

While he has sponsored my season, Lord Wiltshire has made no mention of a dowry or proposed a settlement upon a suitor. Likewise, the countess continues to hint that I should set my affections on a younger son whose family would be content with their improved connections.

The baron is not the only gentleman making assumptions on the dance floor, but I have been content in my position dependent upon their generosity.

Reuben looked up from the pages and battled the nauseating jealousy twisting his midsection. Her mention of numerous suitors was troubling enough, but unlike previous letters, she did not clearly say she wasn't interested in marrying any of them.

Had she forgotten him already as more than a friend?

Or maybe he simply hadn't read far enough.

He turned his attention back to the letter, determined to reclaim his earlier mood.

Now for the most exciting and troubling news of all. Perhaps you can help me to make sense of it.

Lord Wiltshire sent for me this morning to convey the findings of his solicitor. The man had a connection in the War Department who was able to more closely examine the papers found with me on the vicar's doorstep and has confirmed they are a copy of someone's marriage lines. Much of the names are illegible, but there is mention of a location near Oxford.

Based upon my assumed age, the solicitor is now making inquiries to generate a list of potential couples from the various parish registers in the attempt to locate someone with the initials on the handkerchief.

There is sweet solace in the knowledge that while I may still be apparently orphaned and abandoned, at least I am legitimate.

However, my foolish heart grasps for the possibility of discovering distant relatives I might be reunited with.

Reuben's mood soured further.

While the presence of marriage lines with an abandoned child certainly spoke to legitimacy, he could not summon genuine joy on her behalf.

Not when his own heart longed for such proven reassurances.

He folded and tucked the letter away into an inside pocket, then stared across the water as he wrestled with his emotions.

Already exhausted after weeks of long hours installing the new equipment, he struggled to separate joy from disappointment and jealousy from fear.

For the first time since she was carried away to the earl's estate, he was at a loss for what to say to her. Of what to write.

Not when she was slipping through his fingers.

She would see through his half-hearted attempts to be happy on her behalf and he was no longer eager to share the success of a half hour ago.

What was the sale of cloth to a knight compared to dancing with nobility? And worse, there was nothing he could do to change the situation in his favor that he had not already done.

Reuben stood and with slumped shoulders returned to an afternoon overseeing the woolen enterprise since it was all he truly had any control over.

It wasn't until later that evening when she brought out a honeyed cake to celebrate his birth that his mother finally commented on his foul temper.

He sighed. "I had another letter from Kathleen."

"Unpleasant news?"

"Nay. Unless you consider positive clues to her respectable heritage and a line of suitors upsetting." He sighed. "Even with our advancements and the new contracts, I cannot compare with what

Kathleen sees every day. And it's destroying me to hear about her dancing with all those titled men."

"Not everyone there has a title."

"Really? How would you know?" He stopped just short of a disrespectful snort.

She stared across the table with the hint of a smile but a world of pain in her eyes. "Because I married the third son of such a noble. A mere mister."

"You what?" Reuben sat up tall, mentally scrambling over the pages of the DeBrett's Peerage they had studied months earlier. "I do not remember any Cookes on the list." Although there were so many entries, his interest had dwindled when it came to the countless lesser titles.

However, even then, the records focused on those with hereditary titles and not the younger sons who would carry on the family's surname without benefit of inherited income or wealth.

His mother's voice came out in a whisper. "I took back my maiden name after he remarried."

"After he what? You're—" He gasped. "—Divorced and not widowed at all?" Oh, the scandal if the gossips discovered that information.

"Not divorced." She bent at the waist, clutching folded arms over her stomach as her voice broke. "But not widowed either. The papers with the wedding announcement claimed he was a widower so apparently he thought I was dead. Or at least told everyone as much. But the shock of seeing the story brought on your birth too soon..."

Over the years, he had heard other stories about how she'd almost died. The fact they had both survived was apparently a miracle in itself.

"...By the time I was healthy again, it was too late to stop the wedding."

Reuben fought to breathe and the implications of her revelation swirled in his mind. "Did you ever...? Does he...? What is...?" Which question should he ask first? And why couldn't he complete a thought?

She drew in a deep breath, then exhaled slowly. "However, what is in the past, should remain in the past. Just know that often the number of younger sons outnumber the heirs."

Except Kathleen was being encouraged to consider those younger sons.

"Now, if you'll excuse me, I believe I shall retire early." She gathered their dishes and left the room.

Reuben bent his head into his hands as a line from Kathleen's letter filtered through his mind. *Now for the most exciting and troubling news of all. Perhaps you can help me to make sense of it.*

Could she help him do the same?

After all, he now had verbal evidence his mother was indeed married. That he too was legitimate. And yet did she have her own marriage lines to offer as proof? If so, what was his true surname? Was his father still alive? And in the past three and twenty years, why had she never contacted him with the truth?

Not that he could write any of that into a letter that could fall into the wrong hands.

How was he supposed to advise Kathleen when her innocent celebration had upended his steady life?

Better not to write for awhile.

Early April

Kathleen danced along with the others under the gleam of crystal chandeliers reflected on a polished ballroom floor.

Another ball. Another gown. The same musical selections. Same faces preening and strutting and tittering and scrambling for position. Same superficial gossip of fortunes and titles and matchings.

And she was sickened by it all.

Couldn't they talk of anything else? What of the wars their fellow countrymen were waging?

She had felt deeper connections debating Reuben over a point of history beside the vicarage fire than dressed in finery dancing in the arms of a gentleman.

The music ended and she curtsied to her dance partner. A new man stepped up to take his place. However, instead of the black jacket she had become accustomed to, the newcomer wore the red coat of a military officer.

Her smile widened.

At last. Something different.

Except he frowned and kept a stiff distance as if she were just another husband hunter.

After a few minutes, her curiosity got the better of her. "I fear I do not recognize your regimental badge. What type—"

"Rifle Corps." The officer narrowed his eyes. "And soon to return to my unit in the mountains of Spain."

She had read several reports in the earl's castoff newspapers but did not know why an officer would leave the conflict before its conclusion unless injured. But the man was obviously unaffected.

"What brought you—"

The man practically growled, then stepped away from her, offered a quick bow, and departed.

Leaving her alone on the dance floor.

Rejected for asking an innocent question.

Mrs. Pembroke would have told her to confine herself to proper topics. Should she instead have asked about the weather on the continent?

Turning on her heel, she put the dancing behind her, instead making her way outside to the terrace overlooking the gardens. There were a few couples scattered about talking in quiet voices, but all ignored her as she made her way to the stone railing.

Kathleen drew in several deep breaths.

She could not bear to pretend ignorance or hide the same intellectual curiosity her adoptive father had nurtured and encouraged.

After staring out over the manicured paths, she lifted her gaze to the stars above London. The same stars that shone over Yorkshire. Over Armston.

If only she was there again. In the place where last she'd felt like she belonged.

And yet, there was comfort in knowing her dear Reuben could see these same stars.

Despite his silence and the absence of letters recently, there was not too great a distance between them. Not where it mattered the most.

She pressed a hand near her waist and the small pocket in her corset where she carried his pendant. Her lady's maid, by orders of Lady Wiltshire, refused to let her wear the token, but that did not mean she could not keep the evidence of Reuben's devotion nearby.

Music filtered out the door and she swayed slightly to the melody of a scandalous waltz.

Dancing would be ever so much more enjoyable if she were in Reuben's arms.

Her pulse leapt as her imagination took over. He would bow and she would curtsy. And then with joined hands plus her hand on his firm shoulder and his at her waist, she could almost feel the breathless wonder of making the requisite turns in full view of society.

The breathless and heady sensation of gazing up into sparkling green eyes glowing with his resolve and adoration.

It was easy to picture for she'd seen the same emotion in them just moments before his proposal last summer.

Before their first kiss.

Before the accident and her father's written wishes set her on her current path.

Where did she belong?

With her first love. And last.

With Reuben where she could be herself and resurrect their dreams of marriage and family.

The music shifted again and her mind returned to the present while thoughts of Reuben lingered.

As she often did when missing his presence, she began to mentally write him another letter requesting even more village news. Shearing season was likely behind them and if they were in the midst of processing the wool, she would need patience to await a response.

The evening's chill drove her back inside the crowded ballroom where she sought a quiet place to wait out the remainder of the evening.

Somewhere away from Lady Wiltshire's increasing moodiness.

After months of dwelling in their household, she understood why the earl avoided spending overmuch time with his wife. Her conscience convicted her of such disloyal thoughts.

And yet, her primary goal was to survive to the end of the season for Lord Wiltshire's sake.

Out of the corner of her eye, she caught sight of Miss Montgomery approaching with a swirl of her pink silk skirts.

Viscount Lewisham seemed to have rejected his mother's manipulations and left the girl to her other suitors. Suitors the girl had equally encouraged.

Kathleen was tired of the games but maintained a friendly demeanor whenever their paths crossed.

Miss Montgomery grasped Kathleen's hand. "I am ever so excited. Mama has just agreed for me to arrange a house party in a fortnight. Our country estate is not far and the change of pace would breathe new life into the end of the Season, don't you agree?"

An estate in the country? Oh, what she wouldn't give for the chance to breathe the fresh air.

Kathleen sought to conceal her envy.

"Of course, you're invited. After all, my cousin will be in attendance."

The leering pompous fool? Was enduring the man's attentions sufficient payment for the opportunity to escape London even if only for a few days?

Miss Montgomery's wide eyes held a speculative gleam. "Of course, you could not come unaccompanied. Perhaps if Lady Wiltshire cannot attend, they might be prevailed upon to set Lord Lewisham as your temporary guardian."

Her stomach twisted. The invitation was just another ploy to get Lewisham's attention with no true desire to see to Kathleen's happiness.

Who was she? Apparently still a pawn in society's games.

But even if that was how she was perceived, she could not ignore her desire to see the countryside again instead of endless rows of town homes. To be driven along dirt roads instead of jarring and rattling cobblestones.

Kathleen forced what she hoped was an amiable smile. "If you can guarantee the proper arrangements to the satisfaction of Lord Wiltshire, then I would be delighted to partake in your excursion."

A greedy gleam flashed in the girl's eyes. "I guarantee it will be a week you won't forget."

Chapter Nine

Early April

K athleen's latest letter wrinkled in Reuben's clenched hand and he hurriedly smoothed it out.

It was not her fault that he was overwhelmed and on the verge of exhaustion from overseeing and helping to shear not only his flock but others in Armston.

He sat on the dwindling pile of last year's hay inside his barn, then read again the words relating her excitement about being invited to attend a house party an hour's journey from London. While she mostly shared her eagerness to see the countryside again, she also listed the names of the invited guests including the earl's firstborn son.

Why wouldn't she spend time with the young viscount? Or even the baron who had paid her previous attention? After all, Reuben had not answered her letters, likely causing her to doubt his affection and look elsewhere for companionship.

Jealousy clouded his mind.

If only he knew what to say.

He could ignore the surprising and unsettling information about her parents. He could fill his reply with local gossip and an account of the village's growing woolen industry. He could reassure her of his love.

But ever since his birthday, he had been preoccupied with never-ending questions. Questions that had stolen his appetite and restorative sleep.

Questions his mother had avoided by retreating to her room each evening or staying busy in the midst of the weaving activities.

Not that he was any better since he was ashamed of his anger.

Anger at his mother for keeping secrets. And at his father for marrying another and abandoning not only his wife but his child.

It had been easier to let work fill every hour until physical exhaustion guaranteed at least a few hours of sleep before a faceless man appeared in his dreams.

Kathleen would understand and would even attempt to help him sort out how to move forward with his life. But he could not—would not—burden her with the circumstances around his birth. Not with her at such a distance.

He clenched his jaw and tucked her letter into his jacket pocket before rising and striding through the midday mist toward the rear door of the cottage.

Once inside, he found his mother stirring a pot of stew over the fire. She turned with concern in her eyes. "Shall I dish up a bowl?"

His stomach churned and he dismissed the offer as he removed his muddy boots.

"Please, my son. I worry about your health." Her lips pressed tightly together as she observed the changes he had seen in his own looking glass each morning.

"My health is the least of my problems."

She frowned. "I know the demands of shearing are taxing, but you haven't been yourself lately."

"I don't know how to be myself anymore. Because I don't know who I am."

She flinched as if he'd struck her.

How could he speak to his own mother in such a manner?

Burdened with his regret, he claimed a chair at the table. He nodded for a bowl, then waited until his mother was seated across from him. "What you told me before is consuming my thoughts. I cannot do anything about it but yet my father haunts my dreams."

Tears filled her eyes. "And mine."

And yet she had somehow carried on with life and raised her son.

Reuben ate in silence until one question rose to the surface. "I understand why you couldn't contact him as you recovered from your confinement, but why not later? What is stopping you?"

She dropped her spoon. "He has other sons now."

He gasped. "I have brothers?"

"You do." Her broken whisper was laden with pain.

New questions flooded his weary mind. "Where do they live? What are their names?"

"Nay. I won't destroy their lives even for the sake of my happiness."

"But what about my happiness? Don't I matter?"

She grasped his hand and squeezed hard. "You matter more than anything. Except for perhaps my husband and I cannot do this to him without considering the consequences."

His mind scrambled to follow her logic and then landed upon the realization that such a revelation of polygamy—even if unintended—would tear a family apart.

But she spoke of her love in the present tense.

"He is still alive? You know where to find him?" He pushed his bowl aside as fresh emotions stole his appetite once again.

"He is and I do." Her voice cracked. "But I will say no more at present. I can only rest in God's promise that all things work together for good. Somehow."

"What good could possibly come from being fatherless?"

Reuben shoved back his chair, thrust his feet back into his boots, and strode from the house, briskly walking along the river road to expend the excess energy her latest revelations had set in motion.

Somehow he ended up at the church.

Fitting since he was as angry at God as he was anyone else.

Finding the door unlocked, he slid onto a pew and gazed at the stained glass.

"What good can come from this? What good is it to never know my father?"

If his father was indeed the younger son of a noble, then what amount of wealth or position would that noble's grandson claim? What entry into polite society?

If he'd benefited from such connections, he could already have Kathleen...

Except he might have been raised elsewhere and never had the opportunity to meet her.

And he could not fathom a life without Kathleen.

Why did it feel like he was forced to choose between the woman he loved and the father he never knew?

He'd never felt so lost.

Or so desperate for wisdom.

"Vicar Harris, I wish you were still here."

The kind clergyman had taught him so much beyond a knowledge of the Scriptures. Night after night, he had instructed and quizzed, always pushing for excellence. Always holding Reuben to a higher standard.

Like his mother had asked.

Reuben rubbed a hand over his face. Few sought the vicar's counsel as frequently as his mother. Which could only mean that the vicar had known who Reuben was all along.

And while he took that secret to his grave, he had obviously tried to prepare Reuben for something.

Looking back, the signs were there.

Especially the choice of Scriptures he was privately encouraged to commit to memory. Reminders that he was a child of God. An heir of the Kingdom.

And from the book of Galatians...

Therefore you are no longer a slave but a son, and if a son, then an heir of God through Christ.

Vicar Harris had always known what Reuben had needed to hear. Especially as the fatherless one.

No.

Even in the absence of an earthly father in his daily life, Reuben was not fatherless.

He sat in the quiet as the Truth and the presence of Peace settled into his soul. There was a calm assurance in knowing that God was his true Father.

He was a child of the King and that status overshadowed whatever other surname Reuben Cooke should rightfully carry.

He was loved. Esteemed. Valued.

Even without wealth or position.

With or without the success of the Armston Weaving Cooperative.

He was enough.

Tension eased from his shoulders as he let the burden of his unanswered questions fall away.

And yet there was still a longing or stretching feeling inside as if he was meant for more.

God, help me to be the man You want me to be.

With a lighter heart, he stood and retraced his steps back toward the cottage on the other side of the village.

To the only home he had ever known.

To the home where he hoped to bring Kathleen as his wife.

Guilt pinched his heart.

He needed to end the silence.

But the only topic on his mind and heart ventured too close to his mother's secret.

God only knew what the London gossips would do if that information fell into the wrong hands.

Mid-April, Windham Hall

Tucked away in the window seat of the library, Kathleen ignored the book in her lap and stared past the rain droplets sprinkling the glass. Beyond the intricate gardens she had already strolled multiple times over the past three days, the countryside around Miss Montgomery's family seat beckoned with reminders of home.

But society dictated that she could only explore in the company of others.

Which in her case, meant that of the shallow flirts and brash rakes whose collective venture beyond the city limits had freed them to abandon good sense.

Not to mention there was no enticing any of them to step outdoors in this weather. Which left mindless parlor games and trivial conversation over cards.

The interactions she endured were like those in a ballroom, but worse.

And moral boundaries were being stretched daily.

She leaned her head back against the sawn oak paneling framing her reading nook and sighed.

Lord Wiltshire would be mortified if he knew how his son behaved in an attempt to draw the attention of the elusive Miss Montgomery away from Lord Linfield, another young lord of equal rank but greater fortune.

It sickened her to observe her occasional friend play with the emotions of both men for her own amusement when whispers among a few of the other ladies suggested she had an offer from a marquis already being negotiated.

Even worse were their continued manipulations to pair Kathleen with Baron Tattersall who was in her opinion the least suitable of the current group.

Lord Wiltshire had wished to give her a season in London in hopes she might find a suitable man to improve her lot in life. She hadn't found any in the glittering ballrooms.

Only in the country on a quiet village road had she encountered a man of faith and character who quickened her heart.

She clung to the earl's promise that at the end of the season she could return to Yorkshire. And Reuben.

However, with two months of the tiresome social whirl ahead, she had little hope to survive that long without losing either her senses or control of her tongue.

The season was stealing the life from her bones and leaving only weariness.

And loneliness.

She could do little about feeling alone in a crowd, but more rest would only do her good. Perhaps once she returned to town she could arrange a meeting with the earl and ask for permission to cut back on her schedule of events.

In the hallway outside the closed library door, she heard a feminine giggle and the lower tones of a man's voice. Instead of coming closer, they retreated into the distance.

She blew out the breath she'd been holding.

After luncheon, instead of charades with the others, she pleaded a headache and escaped to her assigned bedchamber. However, after a few minutes pacing the carpet, she had sneaked down to the library in search of a distraction. Then while selecting a book, she had discovered the window seat and lingered.

Being around books reminded her of evenings spent with her father.

And Reuben.

It always came back to him.

With a sigh, she finally opened the crisp pages of the new book, she lost herself in the tale of the Mrs. Bennet and her daughters.

Thirty pages later, the rain let up and she stretched the stiff muscles of her neck and shoulders that she had acquired in her cramped position beside the glass.

She eyed the clock on the mantel, then reluctantly stood and attempted to smooth the wrinkles from her skirt. Her assigned maid would frown, but with the expectation that all would dress for dinner, no one else would see her in such a state.

Taking the book with her, she decided to avoid any unexpected encounters and slipped down the hallway to the back stairs that came out near her room.

She was three steps from reaching her bedchamber unseen when a door opened to her right and one of the other female guests gasped. "Miss Harris! Where have you been all afternoon?"

Kathleen held up her book as evidence. "The library."

At their voices, more doors opened and Kathleen moved toward her refuge.

Except that door opened and Miss Montgomery emerged with folded arms and blocked her from entry. "Where is Lewisham?"

Kathleen frowned. "I know not. Despite his father's sponsorship, he does not give an account to me."

Among the whispers behind her, she caught the mention of a charity project.

The truth stung for a moment, but her personal concern focused elsewhere. "Lewisham is missing? And for how long?" She held up the book again. "I lost track of time in the library."

Miss Montgomery's eyed widened in disbelief, then narrowed with suspicion. "Reading? Whatever happened to your headache?"

A true pounding in her head began as the tension in her shoulders spread and tears burned her eyes. For the sake of their hostess, she could scarcely admit she had lied in a desire to avoid the others.

Nearby, someone murmured that no lady seeking a match would think such an occupation attractive.

Miss Montgomery waved a hand behind her at a tear-stricken maid standing near the bed. "To think that I yielded to my cousin's concern and sent a maid to check on your health, only to have her report that you had disappeared." She glared. "At conveniently the same time Lewisham was heard ordering a curricle brought round despite the rain."

Even if Katheen could convince her of the library occupation, the fact one of her favored suitors was also conspicuously absent had clearly turned her surface friendship to dust.

But she had to try.

"I speak the truth. I retired to my room but could not rest so I thought to find a quieter source of entertainment." She cast a quick glance over her shoulder to see a row of curious but equally malicious ladies eager for the latest gossip, then turned back to the woman standing in her doorway. "Once I saw the window seat overlooking the gardens, I lingered. Too long I fear."

A glimmer of doubt flickered in her eyes but the renewed speculation of the others in the hall drowned out all hint of reason.

"Look at the state of her gown."

"I wager she found shelter from the storm in someone's arms."

"I heard the stablemaster saw Lewisham and a woman together in the village without a chaperone."

"Miss Harris was the only one gone."

"If so, what else goes on under the earl's roof?"

Kathleen gasped and turned to face her accusers. "How dare you insinuate such foul—"

"Enough." Lady Montgomery's voice echoed in the hallway and many of the female guests retreated to their doorways to eavesdrop from there.

Kathleen turned to face her red-faced hostess. "M'lady, I know not—"

A downward swipe of a hand silenced her. "I will not be party to such pursuits under my roof. Your corrupting presence is no longer welcome here or around my daughter." She gestured her daughter toward a speedy retreat, then stopped the maid still trapped in Kathleen's room. "Mary, see to her packing posthaste. A footman will fetch her trunk and deliver her to the crossroads within the hour."

Shock stole her breath. She was to be left on the side of the road? Alone? To find her own conveyance back to London?

How completely improper.

And dangerous.

Highwaymen were rumored to stalk the stage lines and prey upon unsuspecting travelers. All matter of unspeakable horrors could happen to her.

Unless...

"Is Lord Lewisham to accompany—"

"No more." Lady Montgomery turned to leave. "May God have mercy on your soul."

Her shoulders slumped as the doors of society clicked shut around her.

Her reputation would be forever sullied all because she had gotten lost in the pages of a book and left her whereabouts in question.

With a heavy heart, she entered the bedchamber one last time.

She laid the book on the side table. "Please see that this is returned to Lord Montgomery's library."

The maid offered a sympathetic glance but kept on packing.

Kathleen pressed a hand over her churning stomach. "I would have liked to have seen how the story ended."

Meanwhile, her own story had added another difficult chapter.

Chapter Ten

Tuesday, Late April, London

K athleen stared at the finished novel in her lap.

While it had been an interesting story and she was glad to have followed the adventures of the Bennet sisters to their conclusion, she much preferred the author's earlier tale about unrequited love.

Perhaps it was because prejudice based on social status alone was too tender a topic of late. Especially after being judged so unfairly with whispered speculations that continued to steal her appetite and her peace almost a fortnight after returning in shame.

She shifted on the chair in the earl's town home library.

Thankfully, the footman from Windham Hall had lingered at the crossroads to flag down a stage and see her safely aboard after she paid her fare with leftover coin from her previous pin money. She had arrived at the earl's doorstep late enough that Lady Wiltshire had already left for her evening entertainment and the earl had been at his club.

After a sleepless night, she had been summoned to give her account for the already spreading rumors that she'd been caught carrying on an illicit dalliance under the noses of her gracious hosts.

The earl had believed her innocence in the matter but had since been kept busy elsewhere with Parliamentary duties and other business.

Not to mention cleaning up his reckless son's messes.

The countess had been less forgiving, especially when previous invitations were rescinded and day after day the drawing room was bereft of callers.

Eventually the woman had taken to her rooms and the servants whispered that she had been tipping the bottle of laudanum more than necessary to sleep.

While Kathleen had desired to reduce her number of social events, she had never wished for it to have been at the cost of her hosts' good names and reputations.

For while she was innocent, Lord Lewisham was not.

If the circulating rumors reported by her lady's maid were to be believed, he had surfaced in London two days after Kathleen's return with a casual tale of being too confined in the country, of taking a drive to the village pub, and of passing the time with a comely wench.

And after the announcement of Miss Montgomery's betrothal to a marquis, Lewisham had reportedly been visiting club after club, drinking heavily, accumulating debts, and citing the unfaithfulness of a woman for setting him on a path of self-destruction.

Yet despite her son's questionable behavior, Lady Wiltshire accused Kathleen, somehow believing that if Kathleen had submitted to Baron Tattersall's advances, then Miss Montgomery wouldn't have cast Lewisham aside at all.

Meanwhile, it seemed the earl blamed his wife for a pattern of indulging their son's whims.

Kathleen could only hope that over time, the wounds would heal.

She stood and placed the book on a shelf but had no desire to choose a new title to read.

No desire to linger in a room that reminded her of her deceased father.

And a silent Reuben.

No desire for much of anything other than to escape the suffocating feeling of London and the ton's speculation.

She retreated to her room and caught a glimpse of herself in the looking glass. Her dresses were beginning to hang on her frame with darkening circles under her eyes.

How had a year that began with such anticipation of new experiences soured so quickly?

London's shine had tarnished.

She did not belong here anymore. And probably never had.

But where could she call home now?

She fingered Reuben's pendant on its chain as she crossed to her precious rosewood box and the treasures it contained. The gift from her adoptive father still cradled the remnants of her past as a foundling but now also embraced a stack of letters in Reuben's clear hand.

Was he her future? Or would the stain on her good name tarnish their hopes as well?

It was not likely that the rumors concerning her actions at a small house party would reach two hundred miles to Yorkshire, but it was best that she be honest. That he hear it from her hand.

And with all due haste.

With determination, she stepped to her writing desk and prepared a sheet of paper.

My dear Reuben,

I wrote before of an invitation to a house party and my desire to see the countryside if but for a short time. If I had only known what a mistake it was to accept. What damage would befall as a result.

Tears welled in her eyes and more than a few dripped onto the page as she bared her wounded heart and exposed her fears to the only one whose opinion of her mattered.

I pray you do not think so poorly of me as to avoid my company in the future. I could not bear your scorn when at last I am able to return to Yorkshire. I know not when that might be, but pray for it daily. As I pray for you.

Yours,

Kathleen

After wiping away her lingering tears, she blotted the ink, folded the sheet into a tidy square, sealed it, and wrote his name on the outside for delivery by the steward. Then paused.

This message could not wait for the earl's weekly packet.

She reached for the quill and expanded the address.

After rummaging in her reticule for a few coins, she hurried down the stairs to consult with the butler about how to send it speedily.

After he assured her it would be on the way to Armston within the hour, she detoured to the library with a lighter heart.

While perusing the shelves for a new book to fill the lonely hours, her fingers brushed across a book of sermons and she remembered her father's advice whenever she had felt melancholy in the past.

Look to our Heavenly Father, dear one. You'll find you are never alone.

As vicar, he had always pointed his parishioners to God.

As a widower and father figure to a foundling, he had displayed a living example of that same reliance daily.

A smile curved her lips. Despite being fully orphaned and transplanted to London, she was still the adopted daughter of a vicar and his wife and clung to the memories of their teaching.

Nothing could separate her from the knowledge of their love.

And even with their distance and Reuben's recent silence, she believed his love to remain steadfast.

Kathleen sank onto a cushioned chair.

Nothing could separate her from the love of God either.

She was a child of God. God's daughter. And according to the Apostle Paul, joint heirs with Christ.

She bowed her head in reverent prayer and let the reassurance soak in.

Peace still lingered when later that night she fell into bed hopeful for the first restful sleep in too long.

Hours later, she jolted awake to the sound of a wailing cry and slamming doors.

Grabbing her dressing gown, she slid her bare feet into slippers and ventured into the hallway as a footman ran by.

The earl's harsh voice echoed up the stairs as he ordered someone to make haste for Oxford and fetch his youngest son home immediately.

What could possibly cause the earl to interrupt a school term that had scarcely begun?

Kathleen made her way to the railing and peered down for a glimpse into the entrance hall and the rush of activity below. Servants carried basins of water toward the drawing room while a maid scrubbed at marks on the tiled floor.

Dark red streaks. As if something heavy had been dragged.

Nearby, another maid drew the drapes closed over the window, then hung a black cloth over the looking glass.

Kathleen pressed a hand over her mouth as bile made its way up her throat.

Someone had died. And violently by the looks of it.

There was a rustling behind her and she turned to catch the sleeve of the upstairs maid. "What happened?"

The girl's eyes darted to and fro before she lowered her voice. "The viscount. Brought here after a duel but no one could save him."

"A duel?" Kathleen's eyes widened. Outlawed, but still considered a means to settle a matter of honor among gentlemen, usually when a woman had been disgraced.

The maid nodded. "He'll be laid out in the drawing room for those who call to pay their respects." She grimaced. "Not that many will come after…"

After the way he had been flaunting conventions and basic morality.

True. Not many would come from true sympathy.

Only those seeking to dissect the grieving family's reactions and cast further aspersions on the family name.

Another scream echoed down the hall from the direction of Lady Wiltshire's rooms followed by a crash as of shattering glass.

The maid dashed away to see to the mistress of the house, leaving Kathleen alone at the top of the stairs.

How much scandal could one family bear?

Saturday, End of April

"A letter for Mr. Cooke. I was told I would find him here."

Reuben glanced up at the stranger standing in the doorway of the weaving cooperative. "I am he." He brushed his hands off and started across the room.

He was expecting a message from the knight's household regarding their contract and yet as he drew near, he recognized the handwriting on the square-shaped offering.

Kathleen.

A stab of fear sliced through his chest.

What news warranted a special delivery instead of their usual arrangement with the estate's steward?

"What amount do I owe?"

"Fifty pence remains."

She must have paid a portion in advance and he easily had that amount in his pocket.

However, after sorting through his coins, he eyed the messenger. "I may need to send an immediate reply. If I pay for your meal at the pub, will you linger?"

The dusty man nodded. "For no more than an hour, sir."

"Thank you." Reuben handed over payment for the letter and a meal, then as the man departed, he too slipped outside and around the corner.

On the river's side of the building, he broke the seal and unfolded the parchment. His eyes fell immediately to the occasionally blurred words as if the paper had gotten wet.

Tears.

His heart ached long before his mind absorbed her words of being falsely accused of impropriety. Of shouldering the blame for not thinking through the consequences of her actions. Of knowing the rumors had negatively reflected on the couple who had extended such generosity on her behalf.

How she hated for him to learn of what was being said about her.

But mostly how she feared the gossip would put an end to their relationship.

As if he had any reason to doubt her character and would toss her aside at the first hint of trouble.

Didn't she know him any better than that?

A surge of protectiveness arose fueled by a touch of righteous anger.

He had waited long enough. It was time to fight for his place in her life.

Reuben tucked the message into his pocket, then returned to the workshop and the small desk in the corner. After pulling out a sheet of paper, he reached for the quill.

Lord Wiltshire,

I had hoped to approach you in happier times than these with more than a fledgling business partnership to stand as evidence of my ability to support a wife.

As you may already be aware, I had a previous understanding with Miss Harris and obtained the blessing of her father over our union. However, circumstances intervened and drove us apart for a season. A season I now wish to bring to a speedy end.

My dear Kathleen has written of vicious rumors spread about her after a countryside excursion. I have lived with scandal upon my name and know she will need ample support to bear up under the scrutiny.

She fears disappointing your generosity on her behalf and fears she may have squandered her prospects in the face of whispers.

I care not for the murmurs of people ignorant of the treasure she is. I would gladly and faithfully pledge my life to hers and will not be deterred any longer by time or distance.

While sending this missive with all due haste, I will follow speed-ily and plan to call upon you once I am in London.

With utmost respect,

Mr. Reuben Cooke

His heart beat at a frantic pace for having declared his intentions so clearly, and yet urgency still drove his actions as he blew on the ink, affixed the seal, and addressed the letter for an address he'd memorized in London.

Now for the postage.

He cast a glance at the others working at their stations to find they could do without his presence for a bit longer. Only his mother watched him with curiosity. He nodded her direction to assure her all was well. For now.

With quick feet, he ran home, retrieved his personal lockbox from beneath the floorboards, calculated the cost of a hasty return delivery, and was soon on his way down the dusty road to the public house.

A few minutes, the eager messenger was riding hard out of the village carrying Reuben's future in his pocket.

Now to arrange his own passage south.

At the rate he could afford to venture 200 miles, it would take well over a week to get to London and back. And with tomorrow being the Lord's Day and travel forbidden, he would have to delay until Monday to beg a ride to Addingham to board a stage.

That left the remainder of the present day to see to his mother's wellbeing and that of his business interests in his absence.

For the first time in his life, Reuben saddled a horse and rode to Armstrong Park.

Within the hour, he was seated across the desk from the wide-eyed steward reassuring him that such travel was imperative and simultaneously suggesting the elevation of one of the other workmen to temporary overseer.

With Mr. Radcliff's agreement to visit the cooperative daily as an adviser, Reuben strode out of the library, his boots thumping on the polished floorboards as he made his way through the grand entrance hall to the door.

His lips twisted with the irony that he was likely the first visitor to gape upon departure instead of arrival.

One might suggest it had been the descriptions in Kathleen's earlier letters that led to a sense of familiarity, but the most logical excuse was his singular focus on her well-being.

On doing whatever necessary to reach her side.

On proving that her love was worth fighting for.

If her letters were true, the luxury of Armstrong Park was nothing compared to the extravagance of London so he had better become accustomed to being around fine things without embarrassing himself as the village boy he knew himself to be.

He took a slower pace back to the village, soaking in the panoramic view only before imagined through Kathleen's descriptions.

What other views will he see over the next few days?

While he was excited to experience many new things, his mouth dried with nerves.

What if the earl denied him an audience?

He shook his head.

If so, he would try again the next day. And the next.

He dug his heels into the sides of his horse and returned to Armston. Once back at the cooperative, he pulled Stephan aside and explained the young man's duties for the coming week.

Stephan's shoulders squared with both pride and determination as he asked several competent questions.

Reuben clapped him on the shoulder. "I have every confidence in you."

"Thank you, sir."

He knew that feeling of accomplishment and was happy to be the one to instill it in another.

When he walked his mother home later that evening, she was full of questions about his disappearance that afternoon and his conversation with their neighbor's son.

"I have put Stephan in charge for a time."

"Because...?"

"I received a letter from Kathleen today." He retrieved the letter from his pocket for her to read, then watched as tears welled in her eyes.

"I cannot wait any longer to state my case. I must go to London to speak to the earl."

"Are you sure there is no other way?" The flash of fear in her eyes was mixed with motherly concern.

Perhaps because he dared to reach above his position? And yet...

"Kathleen is worth both the journey and expense. I must prove myself a worthy suitor and believe that is best done in person. However, if it eases your mind, I reassure you I will do my best not to breech any social protocol." He stared deep into her eyes. "A letter is already on the way. He will not be surprised at my arrival."

"I daresay he will be surprised nonetheless." She returned the letter with a shaky smile. "However, Kathleen will be there if need be to ease the introductions."

"She will." His tension eased at the reminder that while he had business with the earl, there was also a reward at the end of the road. He would see her again.

"I pray God's guidance as you bring her home to us."

Chapter Eleven

Saturday, Early May

Kathleen sat in the corner of the library, tediously plying her needle through the fabric in her lap. Normally, she avoided embroidery whenever possible, but after the dreadful events of the past week and a half, she embraced the monotonous motions.

From the moment she'd been awakened by the uproar over the viscount's death, she had found herself thrust into the unfamiliar role of supporting the earl through not one but two funerals. For before the youngest son could arrive in London, his mother had consumed too much of her laudanum and was found dead.

After speedy viewings, they transported the caskets to Rotherfield Park south of London where Lady Wiltshire and Viscount Lewisham were laid to rest at the beginning of the week. Despite their attempts to keep the bodies on ice to slow the decay, it was too far to travel to Yorkshire and the earl's family seat.

Having returned to London late last evening, the earl and his surviving son were now clustered around the desk sorting through the correspondence and reports that had accumulated during their absence.

Society would frown upon her presence in the room while business was being conducted, but as distressing as it was to be wearing black again, she could not bear to linger in the drawing room where the cloying scents of flowers and death lingered the strongest and brought back memories of her father's funeral.

She glanced at the earl. His gaunt face and slumped shoulders revealed more of his grief than the black strip of fabric tied around his arm. However, despite his burdens, he was staying busy. It was better than drowning his sorrows in drink or a bottle of opium.

After her firsthand glimpse into the family bonds, she wondered if he truly mourned the loss of his often-estranged wife and their profligate son? Or did he grieve the loss of dreams and wasted years?

"I understand all too well your trepidation." Lord Wiltshire rested a hand on the shoulder of his only remaining family member. "I, too, was elevated unexpectedly with our holdings in a chaos of neglect and mismanagement. However, endeavor not to worry for I am here and there are quality stewards in place at each estate." He glanced at Kathleen with the hint of a smile ghosting about his lips. "Now."

True. Armstrong Park was now in good hands.

The earl returned his attention to his heir. "They can advise you in local matters. In addition, I've taken to keeping journals at the end of each day or week—" He gestured to a shelf behind his desk. "—to document any decisions and the reasons for such. Reading them would be like looking back over the past twenty years."

"I will enjoy gleaning wisdom from their pages." The new Viscount Lewisham straightened beside his father, as agreeable and eager to please now as he appeared upon their first introduction.

It seemed strange to think of the young man as anything other than Jonathan or Mr. Armstrong as the servants had referred to him over her past months in the earl's household.

"If I may..."

"Go on, son."

"Would it be acceptable to sell Simon's town house? There is the matter of the expense and debts to clear, but is it wrong to desire a new beginning as my own man? I could stay here and learn—"

"Being with family is important and it would please me to have you close." The earl's eyes shone with warmth, and Kathleen turned back to her stitches.

The expression of pride was one she had never seen in conjunction with the eldest. Even if the circumstances were far from ideal, she was glad for their renewed connection.

The men continued opening letters and making piles and notes as she pulled the colorful thread through the muslin.

Mrs. Pembroke would have been appalled, but until now, the only time Kathleen had worked on the sampler she'd begun at Armstrong Park was when the countess entertained her guests during her at home hours. Any other free time, Kathleen filled with letters or reading.

A strange sound filled the room, as if someone were choking. "How dare he—"

She looked over to find the earl holding a letter with an express post mark on the outside.

He narrowed his eyes at her. "What sort of scandal was your friend Mr. Cooke involved in?"

"What?" She blinked at the accusation.

He read from the letter. "I have lived with scandal upon my name and know she will need ample support to bear up under the scrutiny."

Apparently after receiving her letter, he had written directly to the earl. She bit down on her lower lip. "I assume he means the village gossip about his mother."

The earl's raised eyebrow called her beloved's character into question.

She took a quick breath, then tried to explain. "Older widows are given latitude in a community, but as you are likely aware, the younger ones are often pressured to marry again, especially if they have children. I was far too young to remember when Reuben and his mother moved to Armston but I've heard the report of how she purchased their cottage outright with an inheritance left by a wealthy relative and proceeded to raise her son alone. When she refused offers from both the blacksmith and the cooper, tongues were quick to wag as if she put on airs."

Lord Wiltshire's face twisted as he arrived at his own conclusions.

She hurried on. "But she is far from a loose woman. I have never met a more hard-working or devoted mother. She also took on extra tasks to support the vicarage in exchange for tutoring for her son. Over the years, they acquired a small flock and began operating a loom out of their home which as you are aware grew into the current weaving cooperative you share a stake in."

Kathleen risked a glance at the new viscount for his reaction. The report from the Armstrong Park steward was one of the first discussed that morning.

"And the son?" The earl waved the letter. "What sort of man is he truly?"

"Bright. Industrious. Devout. Loyal to his mother. Kind to all even when they disparage him." She pictured his striking face bent over her hand when they'd parted.

"And handsome as well even if poor as a workman?"

Her face heated and her fingers drifted to the pendant she now wore openly. "His character shines brighter than his eyes, although they are not disagreeable."

The younger man snorted while the earl chuckled, then sobered. "You have become like a daughter to me and I had wanted better for you before this season ended so abruptly."

"While I am obliged once again for the extravagant gift of a debut, even after seeing all that London has to offer, there is still no one else for me but him."

The earl pressed his lips together with a hum, then turned back to his work. And she to hers.

Until a few minutes later, when he opened a report from his solicitor regarding the investigation into Kathleen's waterstained paper and updated her on the results.

Nothing definitive had been found. With so many parish registers to check and without legible dates on the lines, there was also no way to know how long the couple had been married before Kathleen's birth. Not to mention that many young families around the university then scattered across the country as they returned to their home regions and estates.

Kathleen's heart sank.

It was an impossible task to investigate the growing list of possible couples. And that assumed they were even on the right path with the initials belonging to the husband.

Perhaps it was time to let her foolish dream fall by the wayside.

"I am sorry there is not better news. Perhaps..."

She shook her head. "Perhaps it is time to call off the search altogether."

She remembered a bit of her father's last letter: *As your father and your vicar, I must also caution that you do not let any pursuit of your heritage negate the reality that you are already a beloved child of the King of Kings No other title matters as much as that. You are my precious gift.*

She might never know the truth of her birth. But as long as she had Reuben and God, she had everything she needed. Not to mention she had found a substitute father in the Earl...

Kathleen drew a deep breath. "It is enough for me to know that whoever they were and no matter where their path ended, I still had a lovely childhood with the vicar and his wife. I have made it this far in life without knowledge of my roots."

The earl set aside the report with a solemn nod.

Could she press the moment for an additional request?

She gazed steadily at the earl. "I long for the quiet of the Yorkshire countryside instead of the intrigue of society. And with the cloak of mourning, I would be unable to attend any events even with they were still extended..."

A half-smile curved his lips. "I too long for Yorkshire. You know, there had been a time I had dreamed of building my family there."

"I have heard you speak of it even though we've never visited." The new Lewisham leaned forward. "I must say, it is strange to be here without Mother. I would not be opposed to a change of scenery myself."

A gleam lit the earl's eyes. "We could request a leave of absence for the remainder of the Parliamentary session claiming family circumstances. And if granted, we could take the necessary journals with us for you to study. Let me explore the possibility."

Lord Wiltshire reached for a piece of parchment and dipped into the ink pot.

Kathleen returned to her sampler.

Did all things work together for good?

Lately, it had not seemed to be so, and yet she might be traveling back to Yorkshire sooner than expected.

Back to Reuben.

Thank You, God, for small blessings.

A quarter hour later, the butler entered the room and cleared his throat. "A visitor to see you, my lord. A Mr. Reuben Cooke."

Reuben? Here?

With her heart in her throat, Kathleen tossed her sewing aside, jumped to her feet, and rushed toward the door.

Reuben could only hope that he was not calling too early in the day.

But after arriving in London last evening, he had been far too dusty from his discounted perch atop the stage to make an appearance in this section of town.

Yet, even with a night's rest at the modest rooming house and donning the proper clothing for a formal call, he was ill-prepared to face such wealth. Kathleen's letters had described the area well, but he was still surprised when the hired coach came to stop outside the multi-storied mansion.

He took a closer look at the number above the door to confirm the location before disembarking and paying the fare. As the driver pulled away, he turned and for the first time noticed the black drapes at the windows. Visible evidence of the household's grief.

It couldn't be Kathleen's loss, for wouldn't his heart have known?

Reuben mounted the steps with a sense of dread and lifted the knocker, letting it fall with a thud.

Mere moments later, the door was opened by a stiff butler.

The time had come.

"Mr. Reuben Cooke to see Lord Wiltshire. I sent word a few days ago for him to expect me."

The man raised an eyebrow as he examined Reuben's simple garments, but left him standing alone in the entry instead of on the street before disappearing down a short hallway.

Reuben examined the lavish decorations of the home where Kathleen had been living. Could he really take her away from all of this?

And then his eyes fell upon a covered mirror just as a black-garbed woman emerged from the room where the butler had gone.

She turned his direction and gasped. "It *is* you!"

As Kathleen hurried his direction, his eyes drank in the sight of her fashionable dress, perfectly styled hair, and wide smile while equally discerning the dark circles around her green eyes and her too-thin frame.

He had only a moment to register the changes before she threw herself at his chest and he wrapped his arms around her to prevent her from falling.

To keep her close to his heart.

The contact felt like coming home and he never wanted to let her go.

Sobs shook her shoulders as she buried her face against the fabric of his waistcoat and babbled something about the countess and a viscount between hiccups.

He had not seen her nearly this overcome with emotion since her father's fatal accident and soon found himself rubbing a hand on her back seeking to comfort her.

In piecing together her disjointed words, it seemed the family had just returned from not one but two burials and he sympathized with her loss.

Someone nearby cleared their throat. "Mind yourself, Kathleen."

The stern voice had her stiffening, then stepping out his grasp while fumbling in the folds of her skirt for a handkerchief.

Reuben handed her his own, then turned his attention to the older gentleman, catching a glimpse of a younger man with matching hair color behind him. Based on their elaborate clothing, the first gentleman was the earl. The man looked vaguely familiar somehow likely to Kathleen's accurate descriptions.

"My Lord." He executed the perfect bow of deference. "I have been traveling ever since receiving Miss Harris' letter and was unaware until just now that circumstances had altered. Forgive my intrusion into your time of grief." He lifted his gaze and met the earl's eyes. "May I offer my condolences."

The earl gasped and swayed on his feet.

Reuben jumped to steady him.

"Your look is that of my Bella."

He helped the shaken man to a nearby chair while Kathleen called for the butler and the younger man lingered nearby.

A large hand grasped Reuben's arm with a strong grip. "Do you know of Isabella Cooke?"

"I know not why my mother's name is relevant in this situation. As I stated in my letter, I have come to propose marriage to the one who holds my heart."

Kathleen sighed and stepped to his side. "I gladly accept."

He gazed into her smiling eyes. "I thank God for you."

Their moment ended too soon as the earl tugged on his arm. "Your mother's location is of vital importance."

Reuben masked his confusion and humored the man. "She is in Armston either at the weaving cooperative or our cottage."

"When were you born?"

"The sixteenth of March in the year 1790."

The earl's face paled. "Did her family have an inn near Oxford when she was younger?"

"Yes." Reuben moved aside to allow the butler and another liveried man access to their master.

"My dear Bella. I thought... No wonder Peter..." His eyes drifted closed, then snapped open. He jumped to his feet and ripped the black armband from his sleeve. "Philip, have a carriage and four prepared. Kathleen, have your maid pack your things for a long journey. Jonathan, you as well." He nodded to the lesser servant with more implied orders. "We leave within the hour."

Reuben could only stare at the revived earl who disregarded acceptable grieving over his close family and issued orders with such authority.

Lord Wiltshire turned to Reuben. "Where are you lodging?"

Reuben opened his mouth to answer, but was cut off as the earl pointed at a footman who'd arrived in the commotion. "Take Lord Lewisham to fetch his things."

"Father?" The younger man stepped up beside the earl. "My things are above stairs."

The earl paused for a moment then put a hand on his son's shoulder. "It will be an adjustment to be certain." He turned back to Reuben. "Reuben, is it?"

He nodded.

"Hmm. A son. The firstborn. How appropriate."

Kathleen edged closer. "If I might ask, where are we going?"

A gleam lit the earl's eyes. "To Yorkshire, my dear. To find my wife."

Chapter Twelve

H is wife?

After an hour of flurried activity, Kathleen was still speechless at the short explanation.

A heavy silence filled the carriage as they rattled their way along cobblestone streets toward the city limits of London. Another carriage carrying the earl's valet, her lady's maid, and more luggage followed behind.

Reuben fidgeted beside her on the back-facing bench, likely glad to be near her and headed home at another's expense. And equally aware of the earl's constant stare as the man studied Reuben's physical attributes from the dark hair on his head to his long fingers.

She also compared the two men, noticing the similarities in their eye color and shape of their mouths. But how was it possible?

Her gaze drifted across from her to Jonathan. The red-haired, frowning, and bewildered young man who had been eager to learn from his father only to be tossed aside.

The youth who alternated between a pain-filled glance at his sire and a glare at the interloper who further upended his life.

Meanwhile, she was completely confused.

His wife?

While packing, she had stolen a peek at her copy of DeBrett's Peerage. The earl's listing had no name listed for his first wife with just a simple married date and death date, followed by the date he had succeeded his father as earl mere days later. Then the typical level of detail emerged with his marriage to Phoebe Dixon, the second daughter of Viscount Wexley, and the dates of their children's births.

However, she'd always known there was a story buried in there somewhere because not only was Simon born six months after the marriage, those vows were spoken less than a month after his first wife died and he was elevated in rank.

She had heard the speculation from Miss Montgomery's lips directly but knew in her heart that the earl would never have compromised one woman and invented the story of her death in order to cover his mistakes.

Especially when he was currently rushing to the countryside with more joy in his eyes than she'd ever seen.

Not to mention Reuben's birth date fell right in the middle of it all.

Her head throbbed with the questions that needed answers.

And since she was the least emotionally invested in the outcome, it seemed she was the most likely person to uncover the truth.

She cleared her throat. "I pray you forgive my intrusion into such personal matters, but there is a story to be pieced together to ease all our minds. And we've the time on this journey to find such answers."

Jonathan nodded and Reuben relaxed slightly onto the cushioned seat they shared.

She turned to the earl. "Perhaps we should start at the beginning with your youth and when you met my father, Peter, at Oxford."

Jonathan stiffened and Lord Wiltshire finally turned his attention to his youngest, as if finally recognizing the impact his shocking announcement was having on them all.

He sighed, then nodded at Kathleen. "I will start a little further back, if I may. You already know that I grew up at Armstrong Park where I roamed the countryside with my two older brothers."

Reuben drew in a quick breath and held it as the earl continued.

"Thomas was naturally the heir and viscount, so he soon was required to advance his learning with that role in mind. Eventually William joined the Royal Navy as an officer and as the youngest, I made plans to take Holy Orders and assume the vicarage living at Armston."

Jonathan pivoted to face his father as if finding common ground with his father since until a fortnight before, he had been on a similar path.

When the earl's pause stretched, Kathleen intervened. "You went to Oxford and met my father. You told me he witnessed your marriage."

Reuben gasped. "The vicar knew it was you all along?"

The earl nodded. "He knew us both." He turned back to Kathleen as if she were the easiest to talk to. "Peter and I were inseparable for years. Until I happened into a Wheatley inn during a trip to London to see my family and there I met the innkeeper's daughter, Isabella Cooke, and was enraptured."

Reuben cleared his throat. "In Wheatley, you say? The stage stopped there on my travels. My mother told me her family operated an inn but never revealed the specific location, just somewhere near Oxford. She always kept the details vague for some reason. A reason I'm grappling to comprehend."

His hand shook on his knee and despite their company, she laid a hand on his arm to steady him as she prompted the earl to continue the story. "And you fell in love?"

"As the third son without prospect of title, there were no impediments to our union. And as she was a lovely, virtuous woman with a gift for hospitality and kindness, I knew she would make a perfect wife for a vicar to serve our community."

Reuben's mother was indeed all those things. "How long before you married?"

"We could have waited until I completed my training but as we were sure of our feelings, we married in June of 1789 before I began my last year of studies." A nostalgic smile curved his lips. "Those were happy times balancing a new household with my studies. And soon to our delight, we learned our family was to expand. As she was able, my Bella took in sewing to supplement the allowance from my father and stitched garments and blankets for our child as well."

Reuben was hanging on every word. It all added up to the perfect family he'd dreamed of someday having.

Yet something had torn them apart.

And from the dates in DeBrett's, she guessed when it began.

Her stomach cramped. "What happened that spring?"

"It was in the middle of the second term that I received word that Thomas had been thrown from a horse during a hunt and died. Our father suffered an apoplexy and had taken to his bed. Since William was yet at sea, I was summoned to London to comfort my mother and see to the funeral arrangements."

Kathleen blinked away sympathetic tears as Jonathan clenched his fists on his lap. It was all too similar to the sudden losses he—they—had recently endured.

"While her confinement would not be for a couple months, I felt it too far and jarring a journey—" The earl offered a quick smile at the way they were being tossed about inside the carriage as their conveyance gained momentum on the postal roads outside London. "—for her to come with me but as I did not wish to leave her alone, I left her in the care of her family."

"When was that?" The quiet question came from Reuben.

"Thomas died on the 15th of February." Lord Wiltshire coughed. "In addition to the burial arrangements and my father's unstable health, I sent messages through various avenues to locate William who was now the viscount and our father's heir. However, knowing I must fulfill the role until his return, I sent word to Wheatley that I would be delayed."

He swallowed hard and rubbed his hands on the black fabric of his breeches. "Two days after the burial, I received a caller. My brother's—the former viscount's—betrothed. She was upset. In tears. For numerous reasons." He glanced out the window of the carriage at the passing countryside, obviously weighing his words.

Jonathan broke the awkward silence. "Tell it plainly."

It was almost as if he already guessed the reason and was granting his father permission to share the secret with those inside the carriage.

The earl sighed and looked down at his hands. "She was with child and claimed my deceased brother was the sire."

Kathleen tried to mask her gasp as the scandalous admission.

The earl grimaced. "That was not the worst of it for my brother had apparently anticipated more than his vows and already spent the betrothal settlement. There would be no extricating from the agreement without severe penalty and as my father's solicitor examined the contract, he suggested and then negotiated for the substitution of the new viscount as groom to fulfill the terms and legitimize the child." He sighed. "The woman and her family agreed to the revised terms and we sent another message to sea to bring William home with all haste."

He swallowed hard and a flash of pain twisted his features. "Less than a week after new terms were reached, I received word from Wheatley. A chimney fire had consumed the inn and all occupants were lost." Tears welled in his eyes and once again he stared out the window. "I left London immediately. There are no words to convey the gruesome and unrecognizable remains and the mass grave being speedily dug. There were no identifying marks on the bodies but the local magistrate assured me that all members of the Cooke household including their guest—my wife—were numbered with the deceased. One daughter alone was spared because she had recently departed to serve as companion to an aunt."

Reuben made a choking noise. "My mother was companion to her aunt and later received a small inheritance from that same relative. Lady Beaumont."

The earl turned to face Reuben with more than curiosity. "In Kingham?"

Reuben nodded.

"I was not informed of such an altered appointment and the locals were convinced of their identification of the victims. I had planned to journey to comfort my wife's sister but before I could depart, another messenger arrived from my father's household."

Her stomach churned.

"How much can one man bear?" The earl's voice was strained with emotion. "Advanced news had reached London. There had been a mutiny onboard my brother's ship and he was numbered among those who were cast overboard and set adrift. While most of the officers survived, he perished in the wilds. Needless to say, my weakened father did not take the additional loss well and suffered a grievous setback."

His voice wavered. "I left the graveside of my wife and unborn child not as a would-be vicar but as a viscount. My father's heir. By the time I reached his home, I was the earl."

A thick silence descended inside the carriage.

After many minutes, Kathleen broke the gap. "So, in a matter of weeks you lost both of your brothers and your father..."

"And my beloved wife and much anticipated child. My future. I was nothing but a hollow shell with no hope. But there was still the matter of the betrothal agreement and financial settlement to resolve. Estates to manage. Burdens that I was ill-prepared but required to carry." He stared at his hands clasped in his lap. "The lady agreed to a marriage of convenience and an announcement was sent to the newspapers. We were married on the 30th of March."

Reuben cleared his throat. "I believe I should take on the tale from here. My mother spoke little of my parentage until recently when I began to press for answers." His glance at Kathleen reminded her of her letter about the search for her parentage, which must have instigated those conversations. "Only reluctantly, she revealed that my father was the younger son of a noble. She claimed they were married although I sometimes doubted that fact for I've never seen the lines."

The earl frowned. "She had a copy but I believed it was consumed in the fire since they were not found among the contents of our Oxford home when I had servants pack our things."

"I would have to ask her." Reuben swallowed hard. "Nevertheless, my mother finally divulged that she had seen a marriage announcement in the paper and the resulting shock brought on my birth early. That by the time she had recovered from numerous complications, it was too late to contact my father to stop the wedding and that it was best to let things be." He eyed the earl. "Because it would cause my father public shame. She took back her maiden name, claimed widowhood, and later used the inheritance from her aunt to move us to a small village and build our own lives."

The air was heavy with anticipation for his next words.

Reuben swallowed hard. "Despite the pressure of the village gossips, she kept her secrets close. Although I now see why she would not consider remarriage since she was not truly widowed. And if she still had them in possession, she could not have shown her original marriage lines to silence the criticism without revealing your name. A few weeks ago, she said she did not contact you for the sake of your other sons and the scandal that would ensue."

His gaze traveled from the earl to Jonathan. "It was the first I knew of any brothers." He winced at the accidental mention of the deceased viscount and another awkward silence descended within the carriage.

If he had been wrestling with such revelations, no wonder he had not replied to her letter sharing her own gleeful revelations regarding her legitimate birth.

Oh, what a burden he had shouldered alone.

At long last, Reuben continued. "And yet, my mother had one confidante and vigorously pressed Vicar Harris to tutor me. She insisted he impart an Eton-quality education in the country. I had come to think it was because I was the grandson of a noble, never dreaming..."

"Poor Peter to be placed in such a position." Lord Wiltshire shook his head. "I'd given him the Armston living in my place since I had assumed other responsibilities. Over the many years, he repeatedly asked for me to come for a visit but I could not bear to spend time there and made my excuses instead. So many lost dreams. And yet without breaking vows of confidentiality, he probably hoped for a quiet reunion with my Bella."

The earl's eye widened. "In his last letter before he died, he came close to telling the truth. He wrote that his daughter had received a proposal of marriage but there was an issue of inheritance to sort out before a contract could be written." His eyes shifted between Kathleen and Reuben.

Kathleen recalled the letter in question. "He said as much to me as he lay dying but I thought it was delirium since betrothal contracts are rare in the village... Oh." Her romantic hopes deflated. "Since he already knew the truth—that you were Reuben's father—then he also knew I wasn't good enough to—"

"Cease." Reuben clasped her hand between his and squeezed. "Never think such things again. I had obtained your father's blessing... Although, I do recall he seemed frustrated about something in the days before the banns could be read. In the days before the accident."

Lord Wiltshire grimaced. "Even if you were not my acknowledged heir, he still could not in good faith perform such a union before God without revealing Reuben's true name. And in Armston, that would have caused quite the stir."

Kathleen gasped. In all the revelations, she had somehow missed that bit of information.

"What is my last name?"

Jonathan was the one to answer. "Armstrong. And yet... You never truly were. If this tale be true, you were Lewisham since the day you were born. March the 16th, correct?"

Reuben nodded.

Jonathan continued with a softer voice. "You were Lewisham before my father married my mother. A marriage that was inherently invalid from the beginning. Making my mother a... And my brother and I—"

"Nay. Do not say it." The earl turned to his youngest. "I entered into vows grieving but with honest intentions to raise my brother's child and support his would-be wife. Over time, we formed a tentative connection..."

A connection that lasted long enough to conceive a second child, but obviously that bond did not last as each devoted their time to other pursuits. She had witnessed the estrangement firsthand and in light of the rest of the story, it made sense.

Especially the woman's devotion to her eldest child and the depth of her grief at his death.

"You are my son because you carry my blood. You are an Armstrong in my heart even if I now have to draw up adoption papers to make it legal. The necessary formalities do not change my love."

Reuben studied the younger man's face. "I know it is painful to consider such a label for I grew up hearing such conjecture about myself. If I may convey some wisdom from my mother spoken over the years, it matters not where you came from. Only who you become. Continue to be the man you are today regardless of what the mean-spirited may say." A smile formed on his lips. "Over the past few weeks, I have been adjusting to the idea that my father was alive somewhere and that I had... a brother. Now God has given me the opportunity to become better acquainted with you both."

One brother nodded to the other as the youngest accepted both the offer of friendship and his resumed position as a potential vicar. "And I you."

"There be truth spoken here." Lord Wiltshire wrapped an arm around his youngest son's shoulders then turned to face Reuben once more. "I care not what society says. I will not be denied my wife and firstborn."

The resolve in the earl's voice pushed the burden from Reuben's shoulders.

He was no longer fatherless.

Yet she could not help but worry for when the reality of Reuben's new duties and title would descend.

However, the current moment was to be celebrated as the lost was found.

Reuben smiled. "I wonder how my mother will react to know I have found you... Should we send word we are together?"

The earl shared a mischievous grin with his firstborn. "Let us surprise her. Although I wish to know everything there is to know about her. You. Your life in Armston." He frowned. "I just remembered that you oversee the weaving cooperative there."

"With my mother as the lead weaver on the looms." Understanding flashed across Reuben's face. "I daresay she will need to be replaced."

Kathleen laughed. "I believe more than her occupation will change. I imagine our dear Mrs. Cooke... Mrs. Armstrong..." She stumbled to a stop at the further implications of the recent revelations.

"Nay, not Armstrong." The earl's voice rang with pride. "My Lady Wiltshire will make her home at Armstrong Park."

Oh, how the village would explode to know that the true countess had been living among them all along.

Chapter Thirteen

Wednesday, Early May

Reuben swayed as the carriage rolled over the rougher roads of West Riding in Yorkshire. He was more than weary and yet the journey had been a fulfilling one as the truth slowly sank into his bones.

Despite the arduous travel, the days had hastened by in pleasant company.

They had stopped in Oxford the first night before spending the Lord's Day giving thanks and revisiting locations that meant so much to his parents. He saw where they had strolled while courting. Their first home. The bakery that now stood where they had met...where his mother's family had perished. The grave where his father had grieved the loss of his dreams.

The earl had left that plot with a renewed sense of purpose while Reuben was left mourning the extended family he had never known beyond stories at his mother's knee.

"Have we crossed the parish boundary yet?" Jonathan craned his neck, looking out the window at the ever-changing countryside.

"Not quite, but soon." Reuben smiled at his brother's eagerness.

While the man still grieved the loss of his family members, he had happily resumed his hopes to take on the vicarage living once he made up the missed term and took his orders.

"It begins past Addingham." Kathleen had spent much of the past days talking about Armston from the perspective of the vicarage.

Through her eyes and his father's memories, Reuben had a fresh appreciation for the village and the people, many of whom were descendants of those his father knew or saw as a child.

Tingles spread over his skin as he realized again how close he had been raised to his father's childhood. Even the location of their cottage was situated on the edge of the village nearest to Armstrong Park.

Without revealing the truth, his mother had intentionally brought her son as close as she could to his true family connections.

He was grateful for the heritage.

And even more so to be reunited with his father.

A man who obviously had been looking forward to his birth and was still in love with his mother. A man who did not knowingly reject him. The warmth of that acceptance continued to seep into his heart and heal the childhood wounds.

Soon, they rolled through Addingham and Reuben pointed out the various mills and weaving workshops he had used as inspiration.

Those observations prompted a conversation about the weaving cooperative and plans were made for his father—the earl—to tour the operation in the days ahead.

Plans that would have to fit around Reuben's hasty education in estate management and meetings with the solicitors that had been summoned to meet them in Yorkshire by the end of the week.

Now every mile was getting closer to home and his mother.

Little had he known when traversing these same roads the previous week that he would return home in such style. In such a changed position.

How would his mother react?

With the benefit of hindsight, he recalled her expression when they examined the copy of DeBrett's Peerage together. Or before when seeing the earl's carriage outside the vicarage after the funeral.

But mostly her parting words the day he announced his intention to travel to London. *I daresay he will be surprised...However, Kathleen will be there if need be to ease the introductions.*

She had known exactly who Reuben was going to see. Had known what could happen when he appeared on the earl's doorstep. Had known the potential for scandal and rejection, but had let him go regardless.

All to gain Kathleen's hand.

However, while she might have imagined a reunion between father and son, she did not yet know the man was widowed again.

That he was free to marry. Free to step into his former role.

Reuben's face heated to think of his mother being courted, romanced, kept.

Before he could fully process the inevitability, the carriage rounded a bend in the River Wharfe and he caught sight of Armstrong Park on the rise before them presiding over the countryside like a castle on the hill.

The estate was their eventual destination, but first, they had to locate his mother.

The coachman had already been given instructions, so Jonathan could only gape as they rolled past the turn leading to the family seat. However, as they were about to pass his cottage on their way to the old mill building, he caught a flash of movement in the window.

"Halt." Reuben reached overhead and pounded the roof beneath the coachman's perch.

The carriage came to a stop and Reuben was the first to exit.

"I should prepare her..." As he hurried to the cottage door, he heard Kathleen speaking to the earl and Jonathan behind him.

Once inside, he stared in disbelief at the half-filled crates littering the floorspace. "Mother?"

She rushed to his side with a wide smile and peace in her eyes. "My dear, you've returned." She pulled him toward a chair in the front room. "I have so much to finally tell you."

He grinned. Apparently word of the earl's changed marital status had reached the village. "I believe I am now quite aware of—"

There was a scrape in the entry way. "I could not wait another moment."

His mother spun that direction. "Ned." Then with a cry of delight, she launched herself into the earl's arms with a sob.

The action reminded him of Kathleen's greeting a few days before. After they had only been separated for a few months, not years. Decades.

Reuben could not imagine marrying Kathleen then having her stolen from him.

His father held her close, his shoulders shaking and voice cracking. "My Bella. I stood over your grave."

Such genuine love between the earl and his wife. His countess.

Reuben turned away at the intensity of their emotions and the ramifications finally felt real.

He was the son of an earl and countess.

He was a viscount with a seat in Parliament.

One day he would become an earl himself.

With Kathleen as his countess?

He was somewhat light-headed until a warm hand on his arm steadied him. Yes, with her at his side, he could face the future no matter where the path led.

Kathleen led him and an uncomfortable looking Jonathan toward the kitchen, leaving behind the couple and their whispers of love, regret, and forgiveness.

As she had done before during their own courtship days, Kathleen moved about the kitchen stoking the fire and putting on a kettle to heat while he and Jonathan took seats at the table.

His brother observed the rustic living space with curiosity, and then determination. As if accepting Reuben's past and embracing his own future in Armston among similarly impoverished parishioners.

By the time the kettle was hot enough for tea, his parents joined them and his mother took over her duties as a proper hostess setting out a light repast away from the curious eyes of the villagers.

Until his father interrupted her activity to properly introduce her to his other son, Jonathan.

As he'd expected, his mother greeted the younger man warmly. "I am delighted to meet you." Her eyes swept over his face and hair. "You are the spitting image of your father at the same age. And an Oxford man as well. I am sure you make him proud."

Jonathan flushed under the attention.

And then his mother noticed the band on Jonathan's arm and sobered. "Pray forgive me. I did not mean to overlook your recent loss. You have my sympathies in your grief."

Jonathan blinked, then nodded.

His mother turned to the earl. "Forgive me for not extending my condolences, for you too lost—"

"My brother's child." His father swallowed and left the other implications unspoken. They had also lost his brother's betrothed and lover.

Although his mother might not know the full story. Yet.

However, the reminder set Reuben to thinking.

In another world, the recently dead man he had never met would have been his cousin. And yet, if his father's brother Thomas—Reuben's uncle, the viscount—had lived, Reuben would still have been raised in this very village as the vicar's son.

And Kathleen would have been dropped on their doorstep...with them raised as siblings.

Or her being sent to an orphanage in York...

Perhaps God had a plan in it all.

Friday

After months away, Kathleen relished the comfort of Armstrong Park's drawing room.

Even more welcome was the absence of Mrs. Pembroke's critical eye, replaced by the kindly Mrs. Seymour and Lady Wiltshire.

The housekeeper eyed her mistress with curious acceptance while Reuben's mother bravely stretched into her new role as they met to go over the menu and decoration plans.

It was an adjustment for them all, but the countess had opened the current discussion with a willingness to rely on the wisdom of the experienced housekeeper and Kathleen.

As the women debated the availability of quail, Kathleen's mind wandered back to Wednesday afternoon's impromptu reception of the countess in the dining room.

After a light meal at the Cooke cottage—or was that an Armstrong cottage now?—a second carriage had been summoned to transport them all to Armstrong Park. As instructed, the servants had gathered on the steps to formally greet their countess and viscount.

Reuben's mother had insisted that rumors be suppressed from the beginning and requested a meeting in the dining room. Since many of the staff already knew of her from her years in the village, it was wise to gain their support from the beginning.

The earl had been uncomfortable recounting the essential facts of how he had met, married, and then been separated from his wife and child. When the countess brought out her copy of their marriage lines and let them be passed around the room, smiles soon emerged.

Probably because the servants were first to learn of the romantic story long before their village counterparts.

The appearance of the brothers standing side by side assured all that there was acceptance of the new status. And several shed tears at seeing the obvious love of the couple who had overcome such tragedies before being reunited decades later.

Word of the lost countess and heir began to spread and yesterday, when they had worked to fully move Reuben and his mother into the manor house, there had been an audience of curiosity seekers.

While still legally married, the couple had decided to spend time courting and getting reacquainted while the master's suite was redecorated. After all, even though he had stayed there only a few nights on previous visits, the earl refused to bring his bride into rooms that still looked like they had when last occupied by his parents.

In the meantime, plans were underway for a private vow renewal in a few weeks followed by a public reception to formally introduce the countess to the local landholders and villagers alike.

It was to be a grand celebration of the lost being found.

A noise in the entry hall pulled Kathleen's attention back to the present situation as the butler welcomed a trio of London solicitors and showed them to the library.

The library where Reuben had been sequestered with his father and brother catching up on estate business and simultaneously drawing up the proper documents to legalize Reuben as the heir and notify the Crown and Parliament of the changes.

She and Reuben had spoken last evening in the garden of the plan for the family to stay in Yorkshire over the summer and into the fall while he adjusted to the additional responsibilities and prepared to eventually be presented to society.

Would an announcement be placed in the papers before then?

For a brief moment, she wondered at Miss Montgomery's reaction if she knew how close Kathleen was to the real Viscount Lewisham.

Although it was hard to see him in that role.

Especially when her memories treasured the tousled hair of her childhood friend bent over a book and the flash of his green eyes as they strolled along dusty roads.

"Mother?" The object of her affections stood in the doorway. "The solicitors are here and I'm to fetch you for an introduction."

"Of course, my dear." His mother stood and smoothed the skirts of a dress hastily remade from one of Kathleen's gowns while they awaited a visit from the dressmaker.

As Reuben waited at the door to escort her, he sent a quick wink Kathleen's direction and heat flooded her cheeks.

The earl wasn't the only one courting.

Reuben could only sit and watch as his father instructed the solicitors and argued the finer points of the law when it came to the multitude of issues Isabella Armstrong, formerly Cooke's rising from the presumed dead had ignited.

Of top urgency was the unintentional but inevitable voiding of the contracts around his second—invalid—marriage. One of the men was tasked with deeding the property in Hampshire back to her brother in addition to transferring the sum of money obtained from the sale of the former presumed viscount's townhouse as reparation for the inevitable scandal that might blemish their good name.

Reuben glanced at his brother squirming in the corner of the room as the solicitors frankly discussed his illegitimacy.

The situation was already an emotional quagmire without the legal and contractual obligations to sort through.

Thankfully, the next topic was that of adoption papers for Jonathan and Reuben's guilt eased.

Too soon, the subject changed to acknowledging the rightful heir.

Reuben was handed a list of the properties and business ventures under his direct authority as viscount. His father had mentioned them in passing during their journey north, but the written reality was a burden he would need guidance to bear.

And that was before he also obtained a working knowledge of his father's affairs as the earl.

"Better you than me, I say." His brother smirked, then sobered. "I carried the weight for just over a week before you appeared, but am well rid of it."

"You could help…"

"You have stewards for that." Jonathan returned his attention to a book. "I will be content with a vicar's living."

While Reuben had been content to oversee a weaving collaborative. But now he was officially above the same steward he used to seek out for permission in business decisions.

His gaze returned to the list in his hand. To some, the list represented wealth and status. Whereas he was aware of the many people whose livelihoods were bound to those estates and businesses be it servants, tenants, or laborers.

With half an ear, he listened to the conversation about notifying the Lord Chancellor of the House of Lords and presenting proof of his legitimacy to the Prince Regent.

A stomach-cramping reminder that he would be expected to mingle with the social elite next season while voting on matters of national policy. Yet another matter he needed to study.

Perhaps Kathleen would be willing to serve as his tutor.

The final discussion for the afternoon was arranging for the publication of a marriage announcement in the London papers to coincide with the local reception being planned.

That compromise to satisfy the ton's curiosity and minimize the public scandal for Jonathan's other relatives left a bitter taste in his mouth. His mother had been legally married for decades, but at least the locals knew the truth.

And yet the topic was one of immediate importance.

No time like the present.

"Father, there is still the issue of my future marriage to be discussed."

The solicitors already busy preparing the various documents to be signed, paused, and the eldest of them spoke into the stunned silence.

"Your what? There are more complications to sort?"

Reuben focused on his father. "I have proposed and she has accepted. Twice now. And we are of an age..."

His father responded with a slow nod. "Are you sure? Much has changed in your position."

"Nothing has changed where it matters most. I sought to be worthy of her hand before she became your ward and then I appeared on your doorstep to state my case. Even now, I am still unworthy of her character. Even with your guidance and the Lord's help, I fear I cannot do this—" He gestured to the property list and the stack of journals brought from London. "—without her."

"Village girls are made of quality stuff. She has already become like a daughter to me." A sparkle lit his father's eyes. "Ask again and perhaps these gentlemen can carry an additional announcement with them back to London."

His heart leapt at the implied blessing and he jumped to his feet. "If you will excuse me gentlemen..." He executed a quick bow and turned for the door with a chorus of chuckles behind him.

Now to find Kathleen.

Kathleen darted a glance at Reuben walking beside her on the gravel path between the trimmed hedges. He had been unusually quiet ever since he found her in the drawing room and asked her to accompany him on a walk in the gardens.

"Is something troubling you?"

He startled, then a half smile curved his lips. "Nothing troubling at all. Just contemplating the blessings of the good Lord and His mysterious ways."

His words brought to mind her final hours sitting at the vicar's bedside. "I have often struggled to see the good."

Reuben stepped closer and pressed his hand atop her on his arm as they exited the manicured garden paths and strolled toward the viewpoint overlooking Armston. "I as well. Especially in light of recent revelations. However, were it not for a simple village life—" He waved at the town below them. "—and the tutoring of the vicar, our paths might never have crossed. I might never have come to call you friend. Or to love you as I do."

Her heart danced within her. "There is surely good in that." She risked a glance and saw the warmth in his eyes.

But she also saw his new clothes as befitting his station as a man of wealth and property.

A titled peer of the realm with a seat in Parliament.

A handsome man who would be relentlessly pursued by debutantes and their mothers.

Her smile faded. "You deserve a woman of worth from a quality family."

"I have found her."

She shook her head. Society would excoriate him for looking so low. "I have not the education or training necessary to—"

"Nor do I. But we can learn together as we have in the past." He stopped walking, and lifted her chin with his free hand, gazing deep into her eyes. "I don't seek the shallow trappings of ballrooms like you described but rather genuine worth. A woman of moral integrity and compassion. And you, my dear Kathleen, have a heart of gold thanks to your father."

"I may never know where I came from. Or who I really am."

"It matters not. You are God's. And you are mine." His smile grew. "That is, if you will agree." He dropped to one knee and sincerity shone from his eyes. "Miss Kathleen Harris, will you be my foundation? Keep me humble and always tell me the truth?"

She knew their future could be turbulent as he faced the London crowds, but life with Reuben even in London was better than any life without him.

"Will you marry me?"

She began to nod.

"Be my lady wife?"

Her eyes widened at the sudden realization that she would be Lady Lewisham. And suddenly she was the one gasping to catch up to a new role in society.

But the answer was never in doubt.

"I will."

Reuben rose and drew her into his arms, sealing their devotion with a kiss.

Giddy tingles of anticipation sparked to the tips of her fingers as her heart felt like it would swell out of her chest.

They were finally getting their chance.

He released her slightly, then lifted her hand to his lips to bestow another slow kiss over her knuckles. Heat burned in his eyes. "How soon can we wed?"

She pressed her free hand over the precious heart-shaped pendant that already promised his love and fidelity. "Midsummer's Eve is six weeks away and would be fitting, but my heart says as soon as is socially proper."

"Agreed." He squeezed her hand with a mischievous smile. "Because I've waited long enough to call you wife."

Her heart pounded. "With your new station, will we be required to have a society wedding? Because I had always imagined saying my vows in the Armston church."

"I will ask my father, but I do not imagine there will be any impediment. In fact..." A new light burned in his eyes. "What say you to having the banns first read two days hence and joining our celebration with that of my parents?"

She thought of the plans already in motion and how they would be perfectly aligned with her tastes. "I say let us ask for their opinion and their blessing." Her face ached from the size of her smile and happy tears burned her eyes.

As they stood together between the village and the manor, between their past and their future, Reuben bent his head for one more kiss.

She met him halfway.

God had been very good to them both.

You've finished this book, so what's next?

Want more castle stories? How about a mash-up of the Goose Girl and Cinderella fairytales plus pirates set in the Regency era?

Nicholas has saved hundreds of lives—including hers—but can he save their future and restore their home?

(Read on for a sneak peek at the next book in the series, *Finding Home*.)

Or journey back in time to medieval Scotland where the future of two clans lies in the hands of a disfigured recluse and an overlooked second son. You can find Moira and Evan's story in *Stepping Into the Light*.

If you'd like to receive updates about upcoming books or sales, you can sign up for email list on my website at CandeeFick.com.

(There might be a few surprises headed your way including a free novella and other exclusive bonus content.)

Dear Reader,

Thank you for spending a few hours of your time with me.

There is no greater pleasure as an author than knowing that I've encouraged my readers! If you enjoyed this book, please take a few minutes to let the rest of the world know by leaving a review at your favorite retailer or on sites like Goodreads or BookBub. It doesn't have to be long. Just a few words pointing other readers this direction would be much appreciated.

As I continue to write stories of faith, hope, and love, my prayer is that you will experience the amazing love of God and find encouragement for the journey called life.

Until we (hopefully) meet again in the pages of a book, happy reading everyone!

Candee

Preview: Finding Home

Within the Castle Gates series, Book Four

Two hearts longing for home.

A memorable first encounter brought them together, but then Susannah Stanley and Nicholas Pennington were torn apart by circumstances beyond their control. From the Lake District in Northern England to a Moroccan port along the African coast and the Napoleonic Wars in between, they struggle to hold onto hope they will be reunited.

After being supplanted by her stepmother's schemes and the betrayal of a friend, they finally meet again in the most unlikely of places. Now the battle is on to reclaim their rightful inheritance.

Nicholas has saved hundreds of lives, but can he save their future and restore their home?

Chapter One

~June 1803

Today could be his last chance to explore for awhile.

Nicholas Pennington tightened the cinch, then checked to see that his loaded hunting rifle was securely stowed. The valley was home to many a bird, but if he happened upon a deer in the dense woodlands, their cook would welcome the meat.

Turning on a booted heel, he led the gelding down the wide aisle of the stable.

Near the entrance, he caught a whine from an empty stall to his right and paused. A soothing whisper followed and Nicholas peered over the barrier.

"Easy now." Harold, their stable boy, knelt in the straw beside one of his father's prized hunting dogs. Based on her swollen belly and restless movements, they were likely to have pups before the day's end.

At least that would give his father something to be pleased about upon his expected return to Ravenglass from Whitehaven.

Harold glanced up with a grin. "Sneaking off again, are ye?"

"I don't have to sneak." Nicholas frowned. There was truth in his young friend's teasing. "However, if anyone should ask, I've gone in search of game and should return by early afternoon."

With a nod, the lad turned back to his task and Nicholas continued out into the stableyard before swinging up into the saddle. With a kick of his heels, he nudged his mount through the gate and turned away from the impressive castle his family had called home for hundreds of years.

Numerous additions and repairs had been made over the centuries and family lore stated there were Roman ruins at Muncaster's foundation. He found solace in knowing his family roots were buried in this beautiful land.

If only the Pennington name weren't such a burden.

At barely fifteen, Nicholas had yet to prove himself worthy of his heritage.

His father handled the role of landed gentry with ease and after being widowed years before, had diligently expanded their wealth by investing in merchant voyages. But while his father's attentions had turned to the sea, Nicholas preferred the rugged landscape of the Eskdale valley.

Craving the reassurance of the view, he rode up Muncaster Fell, then paused at the top to fully appreciate the sprawling landscape from the shimmering western sea beyond the village of Ravenglass, past the gray stone castle, and then eastward along the winding River Esk until the green valley gave way to the steeper terrain near Boot.

Suddenly eager to see the falls, he turned his mount to descend the hill and once on flat ground again, nudged the beast into a trot. Breathing deep of the clean air, he relaxed into the steady rhythm of hoofbeats muffled by the grasses along the path.

Six miles later, the open space had given way to thicker woods and the rush of water splashing over rocks grew steadily louder.

And above the faint pounding roar of the nearby falls, he caught the sound of singing. He slowed his approach and strained to make out the words.

"I've heard the lilting, at the yowe-milking, Lasses a-lilting before dawn o'day." The sweet female voice carried on the breeze and something about the sorrowful tone tugged at his heart.

The closer he got to the singer, the clearer the words became.

"But now they are moaning on ilka green loaning, the flowers of the forest are a' wede away." A slight hitch interrupted the last notes as if the singer were fighting tears.

Then again, who wanted to think about flowers withering away on such a fine day?

Nicholas rounded a rock outcropping and caught his first glimpse of the musician.

A girl of nearly ten years of age sat near the cliff's edge with a clear view of the plunging waterfall. Her reddish-brown hair fell in a tangled braid down her back, blending with the earth-tones of her homespun dress.

"The lasses are lonely and dowie and wae. Nae daffin', nae gabbin', but sighing and sobbing." The girl paused, then sniffed before wiping her cheeks on the sleeves of her dress.

"Why such a sad song?" Nicholas reined his horse to a halt nearby as the girl spun to face him with fearful eyes. He instantly recognized the daughter of Sir William Stanley and remembered passing by the knight's home, Dalegarth Hall, not long ago.

Did her family know she was out here alone?

He dismounted. "I'm Nicholas Pennington. I live over near—"

"Everyone knows who you are." She shrugged. "I've seen you hiking out here before. I'm Susannah."

"Well, Susannah, do you always serenade the falls?" He looped the reins over a branch, then lowered himself to the mist-drenched ground nearby.

Light sparkled in her green eyes. "Aye." The grin curving her pink lips faded. "But..."

"But?"

She sighed, her slight shoulders heaving. "Today is my mother's birthday and I miss her."

Of course. He recalled the fevers of last winter and the toll it took in their community. Her mother and younger brother had both perished along with a score of others in the valley.

He cleared his throat. "I lost my mother years ago and know the ache."

She turned to face the ravine. "She taught me that song from Scotland. Said 'twas a lament for the fallen." She took a deep breath and blew it out slowly as she wiped at the lingering tears on her face. "This was our favorite spot and so I came here to remember."

A companionable silence fell between them as he soaked in the refreshing view of water tumbling over the precipice into the pool below. Fresh water—like time—flowed on and yet like the rocky ravine, some things remained the same.

Like a child always missing their mother.

He peeked at the girl. "Will you teach me her song?"

Wide eyes turned his direction and pink blossomed in her pale cheeks before she looked away. Such sweet innocence should not have tasted grief.

"I've heard the lilting, at the yowe-milking..." Line by line, she sang the lyrics and waited for him to echo each phrase.

Wishing to cheer her, he harvested a pile of colorful wildflower blooms from among the lush rhododendrons and as the song unfolded, he wove the stems into a crown of flowers from the forest.

They too would eventually wither, but for a time, he prayed they would bring young Susannah joy.

Susannah glanced at the young man beside her and ignored the way his voice sometimes cracked with the melody. His long limbs seemed awkwardly thin but like her father's colt born that spring, he would likely grow into them. But with his thick brown hair, deep brown eyes, and easy smile, it was no wonder the village girls already whispered about him.

She had not been exaggerating to say that everyone knew Nicholas Pennington. And on the rare occasion her father drove them all the way to Ravenglass, she had been in awe of the majestic Muncaster Castle he called home.

What would it be like to live where her precious valley opened up to the sea?

Heat warmed her cheeks and she turned her attention to the last lines of the song. "Sighing and moaning, on ilka green loaning. The flowers of the forest are all wede away."

This time as he repeated the words, she sang along until the last notes lingered in the misty air. However, like her mother's laughter and love, they were swallowed up and washed away.

Beside her, Nicholas cleared his throat. "Thank you for allowing me to intrude upon your time of remembrance." He held out the stems he'd been weaving. "If I may, I'd like to offer these flowers to brighten your day."

She reached for the gift with a smile. "I wondered what you were doing with them."

He waved her aside. "Allow me." Leaning forward, he rested the circle atop her head, then winked. "I say, Susannah, you are as pretty as a princess."

Her blush grew even hotter and the blood rushing in her ears was louder than the nearby water falling onto the rocks.

"However, lass, if you are done with your serenade, I would see you safely home."

She glanced at the sun overhead. "Aye. My father will soon be looking for me." She rose to her feet and brushed the dirt from her skirt as Nicholas untied his horse.

The beast shook its head and shifted restlessly.

A rustle in the bushes behind them caught her attention and she turned in time to see a flash of red fur. Followed by a growl and a glimpse of snarling foamy fangs lunging toward her.

She jumped back an instant before Nicholas leaped in front of her. His bulk nudged her closer to the ravine and her boots slipped on the mist-dampened grass, sending her sprawling and dangling over the precipice.

As her hands scrambled for a hold on anything, she was vaguely aware of the desperate scuffle as Nicholas kicked the rabid fox away and reached for the gun hanging on his saddle.

Her toes landed on something solid and she pushed against it for leverage to stop her slide, only to have it give way. The now-unsupported earth beneath her belly collapsed and her weight carried her down the steep cliff, her body careening off the jagged surface and her left arm being sliced open by roots and rocks alike during her descent.

Her scream echoed in the ravine a moment before she landed on a narrow ledge cushioned only by a few plants.

The sound of a gunshot ricocheted above her and a few rocks fell onto her already-bruised body, trapping her upper body in place.

"Susannah!"

She whimpered, then opened her eyes to stare a long ways up into Nicholas' horrified face as he leaned over the rim of the ravine.

"Oh, dear God. Don't move. I'll be right there."

Since even breathing hurt, there was little danger of movement. Tears blurred her vision.

A scuffling sound above drew her attention toward her right and soon Nicholas picked his way down the steep rocks. As he drew closer, she caught the heavy breathing of his exertion along with a whispered prayer that the ground would hold so she would not fall further.

The reminder of her precarious position on a ledge above the churning water below was followed by an intense wave of pain.

Another moan escaped her lips. Was she about to be reunited with her mother?

However, by the time Nicholas crouched beside her, the agony centered mostly on the left side of her body.

"I am so sorry. I didn't mean to push you over—"

"It wasn't you." She winced as he adjusted her hem over her bruised legs. "I'm the one who kicked away the earth while you were keeping me from getting bitten."

He leaned forward and removed the largest rock pinning her upper body. "We can debate that later, but first we need to to get you—" He gasped as his dark eyes focused on her left arm.

She followed his gaze only to see her bloody flesh ripped open from elbow to wrist. Was that—?

Her stomach churned and she looked away quickly from the source of most of her pain

"Susannah. You're going to be fine." His voice held a strange conviction as he removed his jacket, followed by his shirt. He caught the fabric in his teeth and ripped it into strips. "I can't say the same for the fox."

She caught the twinkle in his eye. "Was it mad?"

"Completely." He wrapped a few strips tightly around her injured arm.

She shuddered to think what would have happened if she had contracted the illness herself. "Then you're my hero."

He grinned. "Never been called that before." His smile faded as he helped her to a sitting position and configured another piece of shirt fabric into a sling to secure her bandaged arm across her chest. "If it eases your mind, the animal did not seem to have ailed for long. In fact... How old are you?"

"Nine years. Ten this fall."

"Well, in a few years, you could make something from the pelt if you wished."

She welcomed the distraction from the pain. "A muff or collar for my cloak might be nice. What do you think?"

"A wise man leaves fashion decisions to the ladies." Another grin curved his lips before he turned his attention toward the cliff. "Now to get you above... I don't have a rope, but perhaps I could ride for—"

"No!" Her heart lurched and she grabbed his bare shoulder with her right hand. "Don't leave me alone."

His eyes widened. "You can't climb with only one arm and neither can I if I was to try to carry you. Unless you can hold yourself on my back, I see no way..." His voice trailed off as his gaze drifted from the remnants of his shirt to their escape route and back to her.

"Please?" Her voice broke as fresh tears welled in her eyes.

He sighed. "I must be as crazy as that fox to attempt this." He shook his head.

"I'm not that heavy and I promise I'll hold on tight and not wiggle." She sucked in a deep breath and forced a wobbly smile. Actually, with her injuries bandaged and secured, the pain was manageable.

Nicholas nodded, then donned his jacket again before trying the remaining strips of his shirt fabric into a longer rope.

Before long she was perched on his back with her legs around his waist. He had tucked the tails of his jacket up behind her as a bit of support and knotted the makeshift rope around them as a belt holding both her and the jacket tails in place.

He slowly stood and adjusted her weight, then repositioned her free hand's grip on the collar of his jacket. "This will have to do. Now, hold on tight with your legs and we'll be at the top before you know it."

She nodded, then buried her nose into his back as she tightened her grip. His chest expanded against her injured arm as he drew a deep breath and soon they were climbing.

Slowly.

But she appreciated his cautious approach even as her muscles began to quiver with the task of holding on. And yet, from her position on his back, she was aware of his wide shoulders and the effort it took to lift them both up the face of the cliff.

Dear God above, give him strength for the task.

Her feet only scraped against rocks twice before he heaved them over the edge and back onto level ground. Nicholas crawled forward a short distance before untying the knotted fabric to release their connection.

She climbed off his back and sat beside him as he heaved deep breaths from his exertion. He had not left her alone but rather gotten her to safety. "Thank you." Her voice quivered. "Now you're really my hero."

He chuckled, then rose to his feet. "Let's get you home." He helped her stand, then led the way to his horse.

"Don't forget my fox fur." She tried to smile, but as the reality of what she'd just survived began to sink in, her teeth chattered.

"I wouldn't dream of it." He put the carcass in a bag, then retrieved the wilting flower crown that had become dislodged when she'd begun to slide and replaced it on her head before lifting her to the saddle. A moment later, he had mounted behind her and spurred the horse into motion back down the trail.

Susannah was grateful for the strong arm anchored around her waist as tremors worked their way up her spine. She'd come too close to death and it would be a long time before she'd desire to return to her mother's favorite spot again.

Which reminded her...

She craned her neck to see him. "I'm ever so grateful you were there, but you never said why *you* were at the waterfall today."

A flash of pain in his dark brown eyes almost turned them black as he twisted his lips. "It was my last chance to explore for awhile. My father is returning today from a trip for business and I'll be required at home. I'd much rather spend time out of doors but his idea of a proper education involves tutors and formal lessons. And many a lecture on what it means to be a Pennington. I fear I will never measure up to his expectations..."

She shook her head. "I believe you will excel at anything you put your mind to. That's what my father always said to my brother...before the fever robbed him of both wife and heir."

Tears blurred her vision once again. Dalegarth Hall was now a cold shell of her former home for she'd lost her father too in a different way. No longer affectionate or quick to laugh, he preferred a retreat to his study with a decanter of brandy over time spent with his surviving child.

Like the flowers she'd sung about, her bruised heart seemed to have likewise withered away.

She shivered, then huddled closer to the warmth of her new friend and rescuer as his arm tightened around her. If only she could stay in his circle of protection, but Nicholas had already turned off the path and approached the stone manor.

Her father stepped out of the barn. He lifted a hand in polite greeting, then halted, his eyes wide at the sight of her.

She glanced down at the blood-soaked bandages and her dirt-streaked dress. For certain, she looked like one who had come too close to the hereafter and with the reminder came a wave of pain.

"Susannah, my lily, whatever happened to you?"

Tears welled at the use of his affectionate nickname and she looked up to see him closing the distance as Nicholas spurred the horse forward. "I fell and—"

"Sir William, I came upon her near the falls and was about to escort her home when a rabid fox attacked. But in the chaos, she slipped over the edge."

"Dear God." Her father's face paled and she longed to reassure him.

"He saved me. Twice." Her voice hitched as she glanced up at her rescuer. "Once from the fox and again when he carried me up the cliff."

He met her gaze for a moment and swallowed hard before looking away. "I am sorry I could not prevent her from coming to harm." He reined the horse to a stop. "She will need stitching. Do you have—"

"Young man, it seems I have your bravery to thank for my lily's life."

A flash of emotion sparked in Nicholas' eyes and then was as quickly gone. After a simple nod, he lifted her from the saddle and carefully lowered her damaged body into her father's waiting arms.

Over an hour later, Nicholas turned his mount up Muncaster's gravel drive with a smile on his face and Susannah's song replaying in his mind.

When he'd set out that morning, he'd never imagined playing the role of hero nor receiving Sir William's praise. After all, there was a reason the man was a knight of the realm.

However, when Nicholas dismounted in the stable courtyard, his good mood evaporated at the sight of his father's carriage.

Harold rushed from the stone building, then stopped in his tracks with wide eyes scanning Nicholas' body.

He glanced down at his blood-streaked dirty garments and tugged his jacket together over his bare chest since his shirt had been transformed into bandages. He would need to make haste to be presentable before greeting his father or else their reunion would be marred by an even harsher lecture and punishment.

Nicholas stepped forward to hand off the horse, but halted when his father appeared in the doorway to the stable. He was too late to avoid discovery.

"Harold. Fetch the hot water." His father turned his stern frown from the retreating stable boy to Nicholas. "Now that he has deigned to return, my wayward son can care for his own horse." With that declaration, the man pivoted and disappeared inside.

Nicholas sighed as he trailed behind with one hand on the bridle. By the time he had removed the saddle and turned his horse into its stall, the boy had returned and activity centered around the first stall.

Resentment burned in Nicholas' chest as he watered his horse and rubbed a currycomb over the horse's withers.

Why would his father pay more attention to a laboring dog than the obvious blood on his only son's clothing? Blood that could have been his own and not that of a young girl?

"I have your bravery to thank for my lily's life."

The memory of Sir William's words soothed the sting of his father's hasty judgment. At least someone recognized his worth.

"He saved me. Twice."

Make that two people who looked favorably upon him.

A smile curved his lips at the memory of the hero-worship in young Susannah's eyes. Even at fifteen years of age, what lad didn't enjoy the attentions of a lass?

And yet, if he had not been out riding that morning, she would have faced the fox alone with far direr consequences.

His tasks done, Nicholas strode toward the exit, then paused by the first stall. "Harold? Where is the stablemaster? I need to warn him of the presence of rabid animals in—"

His father's bark of laughter silenced his report. "Where would *you* see a rabid anything? The only madness I see—"

"I shot such a beast not two hours ago near Dalegarth Falls." Nicholas stared at his father. "During my ride along the Esk, I came upon a girl mourning her mother." He quickly relayed the events of the morning including the fox's attack, the cliff rescue, and his delayed return after fetching a physician from the closest village to tend to the girl's injuries. "I left the animal's carcass with her father if you require proof. I thought the pelt would make a nice muff or collar when she grows."

By the end of the tale, Harold seemed eager for more details, but Nicholas' father only sneered. "If you had to rescue a lass, you should have picked a worthy one, not a common waif."

"Since when is Sir William's daughter considered unworthy or a commoner?" Nicholas folded his arms over his bare chest and glared. "But no matter her lineage, she's a brave child. She cried more today over her mother's death than her injuries. Wait a few years, I've no doubt she'll be the village darling."

With her coloring and sweet singing voice, suitors would be lining up in years to come and perhaps Nicholas would count himself among them.

"It wouldn't take much for her to stand out in puny Boot." His father rolled his eyes. "I've never understood why Sir William would be content with the income from his tenant farmers when there is greater wealth to be found on the seas and in commerce."

Nicholas clenched his jaw and remained silent. There was no reasoning with his father, especially when the man cast a disdainful look at Nicholas' disheveled attire.

"You will never be worthy if you continue like this. It's time you understood where our wealth truly comes from and prove yourself a true Pennington. I was going to tell you over dinner but I've arranged for you to join the crew of the Swan as an ordinary seaman."

"But I know nothing of—"

"Exactly. However, once you understand sailing, you will be able to assist in the planning of future voyages along the trade routes."

Trade routes that might not exist in the next ten years. But Nicholas knew better than to remind his father that since Britain had just declared war on France and enforced a naval blockade, such seafaring journeys might be curtailed in the future.

"We are leaving in the morning for Whitehaven. I will make the introductions and see you off. Now, go. Rid yourself of your filth and have your valet pack your belongings." His father then crouched to pat the head of the dog, effectively dismissing his son.

Nicholas nodded at the wide-eyed Harold, then turned to trudge along the lane toward the castle.

He already missed his home and the picturesque Esk valley, but could not deny the inner tug toward the looming challenge. How long would it take to learn the seafaring trade? Could his make his father proud?

"I believe you will excel at anything you put your mind to."

The memory of Susannah's sweet words lifted his spirits.

If he dedicated himself to learning everything he could on the journey, within a year, he'd be back home and have regained his father's approval.

Get the rest of *Finding Home* today.

More Fiction

A complete and up-to-date list of all my books can be found
on my website at CandeeFick.com

Standalone Romance

Catch of a Lifetime (Cassie and Reed)

The Wardrobe Series

(Contemporary romance in theater settings)
Dance Over Me (Dani and Alex)

Focus on Love (Liz and Ryan)
Sing a New Song (Gloria and Nick)
A Picture Perfect Christmas (Liz and Ryan continued)
Home For Christmas (Grace and Tyler)
Complete Series Boxed Set

Within the Castle Gates Series

(Historical romance in various time periods)
Stepping Into the Light (Moira and Evan)
To Win Her Heart (Emma and Grayson)
The Lost Heir (Kathleen and Reuben)
Finding Home (Susannah and Nicholas)
Saving Grace (contemporary - Grace and Drew)
A Castle in the Clouds (Miranda and Josh)
Books 1-4 Boxed Set

About Candee

Candee Fick is a multipublished, award-winning author. She is also the wife of a high school football coach and the mother of three children, including a daughter with a rare genetic syndrome. When not busy writing, editing, or coaching other authors, she can be found exploring the great Colorado outdoors, indulging in dark chocolate, and savoring happily-ever-after endings through a good book.

Visit her website at CandeeFick.com where you can find out about her latest releases and sign up for her email list.

www.ingramcontent.com/pod-product-compliance
Lightning Source LLC
Chambersburg PA
CBHW022119170626
46808CB00002B/779